Never rely on physical chemistry between yourself and a man. Sexual attraction is fleeting...

Tonight, Elise was going to put her plan into action and find a husband. But then she shifted her gaze.

Goodness!

It was a new face. And a nice one at that. He looked to be mid- to late thirties. He was a natural, sun-bleached blonde with one of those bad-boy haircuts. His face was suntanned, but she doubted it came from a bottle or a tanning bed. He had a good build, but she could tell he wasn't a gym rat. And he was wearing a well-fitted tux.

He turned and made eye contact with Elise. She was surprised to feel the warmth of a blush on her cheeks. The Adonis was looking right at her, a twitch of amusement on his sensuous lips.

She couldn't take her eyes off him.

Then, suddenly, he was coming her way.

Dear Reader,

April showers are bringing flowers—and a soul-stirring bouquet of dream-come-true stories from Silhouette Romance!

Red Rose needs men! And it's up to Ellie Donahue to put the town-ladies' plans into action—even if it means enticing her secret love to return to his former home. Inspired by classic legends, Myrna Mackenzie's new miniseries, THE BRIDES OF RED ROSE, begins with Ellie's tale, in *The Pied Piper's Bride* (SR #1714).

Bestselling author Judy Christenberry brings you another Wild West story in her FROM THE CIRCLE K miniseries. In *The Last Crawford Bachelor* (SR #1715), lawyer Michael Crawford—the family's last single son—meets his match...and is then forced to live with her on the Circle K!

And this lively bunch of spring stories wouldn't be complete without Teresa Carpenter's *Daddy's Little Memento* (SR #1716). School nurse Samantha Dell reunites her infant nephew with his handsome father, only to learn that if she wants to retain custody then she's got to say, "I do"! And then there's Colleen Faulkner's *Barefoot and Pregnant?* (SR #1717), in which career-woman Elise Montgomery has everything a girl could want—except the man of her dreams. Will she find a husband where she least expects him?

All the best,

Mavis C. Allen
Associate Senior Editor

Please address questions and book requests to:
Silhouette Reader Service
U.S.: 3010 Walden Ave., P.O. Box 1325, Buffalo, NY 14269
Canadian: P.O. Box 609, Fort Erie, Ont. L2A 5X3

Barefoot and Pregnant?

COLLEEN FAULKNER

SILHOUETTE *Romance*®

Published by Silhouette Books

America's Publisher of Contemporary Romance

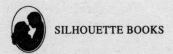 SILHOUETTE BOOKS

ISBN 0-373-19717-9

BAREFOOT AND PREGNANT?

Copyright © 2004 by Colleen Faulkner

This edition published by arrangement with Harlequin Books S.A.

® and TM are trademarks of Harlequin Books S.A., used under license. Trademarks indicated with ® are registered in the United States Patent and Trademark Office, the Canadian Trade Marks Office and in other countries.

Visit Silhouette at www.eHarlequin.com

Printed in U.S.A.

Books by Colleen Faulkner

Silhouette Romance

A Shocking Request #1573
Barefoot and Pregnant? #1717

COLLEEN FAULKNER

had romance writing encrypted in her genetic code. her mother, Judith E. French, is also a bestselling historical romance author. Whether through genes or simply karma, Colleen began her writing career early. She published her first historical romance at the tender age of twenty-four. Since then she has sold twenty-three historical romance novels, five contemporary romances and six novellas.

Colleen resides in southern Delaware with her husband of twenty years, their four children, a Bernese Mountain dog named Duncan and a Siamese cat named Xena. When she's not writing, Colleen enjoys playing racquetball and volleyball, coaching girls' softball and coed soccer and, of course, reading.

THE HUSBAND FINDER
FIRST DATE CHECKLIST
Name of Date: _Zane Keaton_

	Criteria	Description	Score
1	First Impression	Coldly professional (10 points) Common goals (7.5 points) Instant chemistry (5 points)	Knocked my stockings off - 5 pts.
2	Career	Professional man (10 points) Business owner (7.5 points) Other (5 points)	Chicken farmer? - 3 pts
3	Activity	Dinner (10 points) Dancing (7.5 points) Movie (5 points)	Moonlit stroll on the beach - 2 pts.
4	Car	Luxury car (10 + 5 points) Imported sedan (10 points) Sport utility vehicle (5 points)	Beat-up, pickup truck - 0 pts.
5	Zane Keaton	6'1", blond hair, blue eyes Former bad boy with a heart of gold	Perfect!

Final Score: 10 points

Prologue

Elise Montgomery hit the print button on the copy machine in the lounge of Waterfront Realty in Southern Delaware where she worked and perched one hand on her hip to wait. As the machine clicked and whirred, she caught a glimpse of her best friend walking down the hall. "Liz, got a sec?" she called.

Liz backed up, checking her wristwatch. They were dressed similarly in gabardine skirts and jackets with white silk shells beneath. Elise's "power suit" was a soft salmon; Liz was wearing navy.

"I've got ten minutes," Liz said. "New clients coming in to look at the condos at Mallory Bay."

Elise grabbed one of the copies the machine had spit out. "Here we go. The checklist I was telling you about that I found in that book."

"Not another self-help book." Liz lifted a skeptical eyebrow as she picked up a book from beside the copier and read the spine. *"The Husband Finder?"*

Elise shrugged. "So it has a bad title, listen to this." She opened it to the first chapter. "According to the author... 'Women today spend more time researching the cars they purchase than the men they marry. When an educated, career-oriented woman of the new millennium buys a car, she makes a list of the qualities she is looking for such as good value for the money, gas mileage, aesthetics, etc. Then, she test drives various cars and rates them according to her list of requirements. She purchases the car that best suits her. A woman should seek a husband in the same logical manner.'"

"You've got to be kidding me," Liz muttered. "Like buying a car?"

Elise set down the book. "It's a perfectly valid observation, when you think about it, Liz. Now, I've made a copy of the suggested checklist for each of us." She leaned against the copier as she indicated the high points with a pen. "There are various headings and subheadings. You fill in the qualities you're looking for—the author makes suggestions—and then you just total up the numbers!"

Liz stared at the photocopy.

"The fact of the matter is," Elise explained, "we don't have time for men who aren't good candidates for long-term relationships."

"You mean for marriage." Liz studied the sheet.

"Let's see, type of car—sports car, sport utility, sedan. Bonus for cars costing more than forty K. Good. I love a man who drives a nice car."

Elise laughed. "Seems a bit much, but I guess that's important to some people. And it *can* indicate a man's education and socioeconomic status."

"First date," Liz continued to read. "Check one— dinner, dinner and dancing, movie and dinner. Topics of conversation—talks about you, talks about himself, knows what's going on in the world. No clue." She laughed looking up at Elise. "And this book said this would work? You can find a husband with this thing?"

Elise shrugged. "Well, nothing's guaranteed of course, but this is essentially what dating services do, right? And the book is full of lots of helpful suggestions. I've already started highlighting some of them." She paged through the volume to show where she had used a lavender highlighter.

Liz still looked unconvinced.

Elise poked her in the side. "Come on, where's your sense of adventure? This'll be fun."

Liz groaned and put out her hand. "Lay it on me."

Elise handed her friend the checklist. "Now be sure to fill out all of your requirements, then make photocopies. Use one set of sheets per date. There's a place to put his name right at the top."

Liz was still chuckling as she accepted the checklist. "You've had some crazy ideas before, Elise, but this one—"

"Hey, checklists work in the real estate business, don't they?" She indicated the plush office building with a sweep of her hand. "It's how things get accomplished around here. We set goals. We check them off and we end up achieving what we set out to do. It's good time management. *The Husband Finder* is nothing more than a tool to help us get what we want. To help us be happy, healthy women."

"Now you sound like that book." Liz clutched the sheet to her chest. "Okay, I surrender. I'll try your checklist." She rolled her eyes. "Nothing else has worked. Blind dates. Dating services. Personal ads. What have I got to lose?"

"That a girl." Elise smiled as she tapped her on the back with her copies. "Just trust me. This is going to work."

"Gotta run." Liz waved. "Talk to you later."

Elise watched as she disappeared down the hall, her navy pumps tapping on the hardwood floor. "Don't forget Friday night, that benefit dinner," she called after her friend.

"Pick you up at six."

Elise glanced down at the photocopies cradled in her arms. A checklist for potential husbands. It *was* crazy...wasn't it?

Desperate was more like it.

After years of casual dating and no long-term relationships that ever led anywhere, Elise realized she was ready to get serious. She had all the things she thought would make her happy: a well-paying job, a great condo, a good retirement plan. But it wasn't enough.

Her father, Edwin Montgomery of *the* oil Montgomerys of Dallas had always told her that good hard work was the only thing a person could depend on. He had drilled into her head since she was a child that her career was what was important; personal happiness was inconsequential. So for a long time, Elise lived that life. And for a while, her career *was* enough. Only, over the past few months…year if she was honest with herself…her job hadn't been enough. It just hadn't been fulfilling in the way it once had been; she wasn't even sure she liked the real estate business. She realized she was lonely and she didn't want to end up like her father, alone and cantankerous. Elise ached for an intimate relationship with a man. She wanted a partner to love, a man who she could trust, who would love and trust her in return.

She glanced at the checklists cradled in her arms. It was worth a shot, wasn't it?

Chapter One

*Never rely on physical chemistry between your-
self and a man. Sexual attraction is fleeting.*

Elise lifted her glass to her lips and sipped her tonic
water with a twist as she gazed at the hotel's reception
room filled with local hospital employees and bene-
factors. She'd dressed carefully this evening in her
favorite "little black dress" and wore a new shade of
lipstick called *Seduction*. It looked like a soft pink to
her, but she supposed that when you paid $35.00 for
a tube of lipstick, the manufacturers couldn't just call
it *Pink*.

Ordinarily, Elise hated these kinds of affairs, but
Waterfront Realty had bought her the expensive ticket

for the benefit. It was her job to smile, sip tonic water and shmooze, looking for potential clients. She'd been to so many of these events in the past few years that she knew the drill by heart. She would make light conversation with people she didn't know. Then she would push dry chicken and overcooked green beans around on her plate, listen to a dull speech and then go home to have a bag of popcorn for dinner and watch a late-night talk show.

But tonight was different. She could feel it from the top of her recently foiled head to the tips of her new pumps. Tonight was going to be different. She was going to date men, fill out the form, add the scores and find a husband.

Elise spotted Liz Jefferson coming toward her in a way-too-tight black dress. She was drinking a glass of wine and probably not her first. Elise admired Liz's ability to hold her liquor. Elise never drank in public, not because she had anything against alcohol, but because it made her act stupid. One drink and she was telling anyone who would listen how she had always wanted a puppy as a child and had never been able to have one because it might soil her father's white carpet.

At that moment, it occurred to Elise that she had white carpet in her condo.

And no dog.

How had her life gotten so far from what she had wanted it to be? She had always sworn she wouldn't be like her father. Was that who she was becoming?

"Hey, babe." Liz glided over. Elise guessed her dress was too tight to allow her to walk.

"Seen anyone with potential?" Liz parked beside Elise and swirled her Chardonnay, gazing over the rim of the glass into the room.

"Same old, same old, so far," Elise said.

There were men in tuxes everywhere. Elise knew many of them. She had dated quite a few. There was Joe Kanash, who revealed sheepishly to Elise after two dates that he was not *quite* divorced. Then there was Bobby Rent. He slurped his lobster bisque and whistled through his nose whenever he got nervous, which she discovered was often. Then, of course, there was Alex Bortorf the proctologist, Mark Wrung the department store owner—the list was endless. Some of the men both Elise and Liz had dated, though, thankfully, never at the same time.

Elise sighed. Now that she was here, she was beginning to get cold feet. How was this self-help book better than any other? She ought to just go home now and start popping popcorn for her usual late-night date with Letterman. Besides, her new pumps were hurting her feet.

"Hey, hey, hey," Liz said lifting her hand to her hip to pose. "A new face at one o'clock. No ring on his finger."

Liz was better than Elise at recognizing the married ones. Elise shifted her gaze as she raised her glass, but she didn't drink. *Goodness.* It was a new face. And a nice one at that. The man taking a canapé from a waiter's tray looked to be mid- to late-thirties. He was a natural, sun-bleached blonde with one of those bad-boy haircuts. Just a little long at the ears and the nape of the neck. His face was suntanned, but she doubted it came from a bottle or a tanning bed. He was tall, but not overly so. Maybe six foot, six-one. He had a good build, but she could tell he wasn't a gym rat. His tux fit so well that it had to be his and not one of those rented ones that would have to be back at the dry cleaners by noon tomorrow.

The man turned and made eye contact with Elise. She was surprised to feel the warmth of a blush on her cheeks. She hadn't realized she still could blush.

Liz elbowed her. "Hey, I had dibs. I spotted him first."

The Adonis looked right at Elise, a twitch of amusement on his sensuous lips. She wondered if he had caught what Liz said or he was just used to single, desperate women gaping at him.

Elise couldn't take her eyes off him. Then, suddenly he was coming her way. She wasn't sure if she wanted to run away or open her arms to him.

The blonde walked right up. "Hi," he said, halting in front of her.

Elise gripped her glass. She'd met a million men in her life. It seemed as if she'd dated most of them. What was it about this one that suddenly left her speechless? Usually she was so good at causal conversation.

She smiled back and managed a "Hi."

"Name's Zane, Zane Keaton." He offered his hand.

Liz glanced at Elise, at Zane and back at Elise again. "I can see there's no need for me to even bother to introduce myself," she said glibly as she glided away. "Later, babe."

Zane still held Elise's gaze as she shook his hand. She laughed, unable to help herself. "Okay," she said. "I'm definitely embarrassed. I usually play a little harder to get than this."

"Me, too."

"I didn't mean to stare. I'm Elise Montgomery."

"Nice to meet you. Your friends call you Ellie?"

She cocked her head. "Actually, no one ever has."

It was his turn to laugh. "Well, you look like an Ellie to me."

Out of any other stranger's mouth, his words would have sounded ridiculous to Elise. At the very least, a really bad pickup line. But she was oddly flattered. She didn't feel like an Ellie, but secretly she had always wished she could be one. To Elise, an Ellie was relaxed. Carefree. As the daughter of Edwin Montgomery, she had never felt like she was, either.

"So, you come to this kind of thing often?" Zane stood beside her, gazing out at the room.

"Way too often," she confessed.

"Me, too. I hate 'em." He chuckled. "I was supposed to be here with a date, but she bailed on me at the last minute."

She noted that he said *date* and not *girlfriend.* "Flu?"

"That," he confessed, "or an aversion to bad hors d'oeuvres, long boring speeches and dry chicken."

Elise tipped back her head and laughed louder than she really should have. A man and a woman, both dressed in black standing nearby glanced their way.

Elise covered her mouth, embarrassed. "Everyone's going to think I've had one too many," she whispered. "Don't make me laugh like that."

He grinned. "What's the point in living if you can't have a good belly laugh every once in a while?"

She glanced at him. Was this guy for real? Good-looking, charming and funny? She eyed his left hand. Liz said there was no ring, but she double-checked to be sure there was no white telltale ring of skin where a wedding band normally rested. Negative.

"So if your date bailed, why did you still come?"

He met her gaze, his eyes sparkling. He just seemed like such a happy guy. A guy who was happy with himself. A girl didn't see that often in the dating world.

"It was my sister, Meagan, who was supposed to come with me. Our grandfather was one of the major contributors when this hospital was being built in the sixties." He lifted one broad shoulder. "He's in a nursing home now and can't get to things like this. I come for him. Bring his donation check. Say hi."

That was so sweet that for a moment Elise didn't know what to say. A man with family ties? A man who cared about the previous generations? Elise had never even known any of her grandparents. "It was nice of you to come in his place."

"Yeah," Zane sighed. "But I just told Pops I would come, not that I'd stay. I've been here an hour, shook hands with everyone on the board. Ate several little balls of what, I have no idea and now I'm bored. Time to hit the road. How about you?" He lifted a brow.

He was just a little cocky, but not obnoxiously so. In a world of mamby-pamby beta males, could this possibly be the last alpha wolf in the pack? She resisted a smile. "There's still the dry chicken and the boring speech to get through."

He nodded. "You're absolutely right. We could go into the dining room and saw on that chicken. We could yawn through the speeches, or..." His tone changed as if he had some secret to share only with her.

"Or?" she murmured, transfixed by his gaze.

"Or, we could slip out the back and take a walk on the beach. If you're hungry, I'll buy you a cheeseburger when I take you home. I know a great little dive."

Elise stared at him in disbelief for a moment. Slip out of here? She'd spent more than an hour getting ready for this affair. She'd bought new shoes and *Seduction* lipstick. Waterfront Realty had paid five hundred dollars for her to see and be seen here tonight. Elise couldn't just walk out...could she?

Well, her company hadn't really paid for the chicken, had they? Their check had been a donation to fund the new maternity wing.

A smile played on her lips. To sneak out would be totally out of character for her. Elise Montgomery always went by the book. She always followed the rules, and the rules were that if your boss paid five hundred dollars for bad chicken, you ate it. But she could already tell that Zane Keaton was not a man who played by the rules.

"Ah, you found her, Zane." Richard Milton, a prominent local attorney, approached them.

Zane lifted a brow.

"Elise Montgomery, the real estate agent I was telling you about. You want to make a large land purchase in this county, she's the person to know."

Elise felt her face grow warm with embarrassment.

"You're a real estate agent?" Zane asked looking to her, as if he didn't quite believe the attorney.

She nodded. "That's right."

"Well, I'll leave you two kids alone. Call me if Elise finds what you're looking for." Richard walked away.

Elise smiled at Zane. "So you're looking for land."

He lifted a broad shoulder. "Maybe. So, you still game?"

"Game?" she asked.

"For getting out of here." He pointed to the door. "Come on, Ellie, it'll be fun," he whispered when she didn't answer right away. His breath was warm in her ear. The chemistry was wicked. "And just a little naughty. Tell me you like to be naughty once in a while."

She looked at him in wide-eyed surprise and he winked.

The man winked…it was like right out of an old black-and-white movie she liked to watch on Sunday afternoons when she should be working.

"Okay," she exhaled, tantalized by the thought of just walking out. "But I need to tell my friend Liz that I'm going. She gave me a ride here."

He took her empty glass from her hand and placed it on the tray of a passing waiter. "Tell her you won't need a ride home." He pointed at her. "Now I'm giving you two minutes to meet me at the door. Then we make our getaway."

Elise watched Zane walk away, feeling a little numb. Was this the night she had dreamed of since she was little girl, tucked in at night by a nameless nanny?

She found Liz at the bar. "I won't need that ride home."

Liz grinned. "How's he coming on that checklist of yours?"

"Too early to say," Elise confided. Inside her chest her heart was pounding. Her pulse fluttered. She couldn't remember the last time a man had made her feel this way.

Liz nodded with a conspiratory look. "Call you later," she mouthed.

Elise made a beeline for the door, her black clutch purse tucked under her arm. She couldn't believe she was doing this. She *did* feel naughty and she had to admit, the feeling was wonderful.

Zane was waiting for her just outside the hotel's reception area. He offered her his elbow. His smile made her feel like a million bucks.

"I figure we'll make a grand exit," he said as he strode forward, his chin high as if they were royalty. "We get out on the beach and we throw our shoes into the dunes and make a run for the water."

Elise laughed. "I can't really walk on the beach. I'm wearing hose."

He opened the door that led onto the hotel's veranda. "Hose, shmose. Take them off."

Take them off? Elise felt as if her brain was on overload. Stand on one foot and peel her panty hose off on a public beach?

Zane led her across the hotel's Victorian-style veranda and down the steps that led to the white sand beach. "Okay, twenty questions."

"What?"

"Let's play twenty questions. Well, my version." He walked around to the back of the staircase and kicked off one shoe and then the other. "I ask a question. I give you my answer and then you give me yours."

She gingerly removed one high-heeled leather shoe

and then the other. The feel of the sand through her hose on her feet was deliciously warm. "What kind of questions?" she asked suspiciously. Usually on first dates—and she figured she could classify this as a date—she stuck to safer conversations such as where she went to college and what the NASDAQ was doing.

"Easy stuff," Zane said. "Like your favorite color. Mine's black."

"Black? Black's not a color."

"Sorry. It's my answer. Black is my favorite color. Let's see, black like a moonless night. Black like the backside of a penguin. Yours?"

She laughed. "Mine's green." She paused. "Green like a man's face after he's tasted his mother-in-law's potato salad."

He laughed. "Now you're getting the hang of it. Come on." He opened and closed one hand. "Off with the hose. I swear, I don't know how you women wear those things."

She grabbed the rail of the step, then hesitated. Did she put her hands under her skirt, or try to wiggle the waistband down through the material of the dress?

Zane spun around, presenting his back to her. "Go ahead. Do what you have to do get them off. No one's looking." He made himself busy rolling up his pant legs.

Elise took a deep breath and reached under her dress and grabbed the waistband of her hose. She gave a yank, got them down around her thighs and lifted one foot. "Whoa!" She swayed as she lost her balance in the soft sand.

Zane caught her before she went down, his eyes comically squeezed shut. "Got ya."

Using Zane's muscular forearm to balance herself, she quickly slipped out of the hose. "Done," she said as proud of herself as if she'd just sold a half-million dollar piece of property. She stuffed the hose into her pumps.

"Ready?" he asked.

She nodded.

He grabbed her hand and pulled her along. "Okay, question number two. "Chocolate or vanilla ice cream?"

"Soft serve?"

He grinned.

"Swirl."

"Definitely swirl," he agreed. "I like you already."

As they walked across the beach toward the water, they covered questions three and four. By the time they reached the edge of the cool, frothing ocean, Elise wanted a turn at asking the questions. "Okay," she said laughing at his last answer. "Here you go, favorite sport to watch. Mine's baseball."

He looked at her, with obvious surprise as they started north up the beach. "Not ice skating? All the women I've ever known like ice skating."

"Orioles fan since birth, with or without Cal Ripken, Jr."

"You want to get married?" he asked.

She laughed. He was kidding of course, but she still felt a trill of excitement. Obviously he wasn't a man completely against the idea of the institution of marriage. "Another," she begged.

"Cap'n Crunch cereal with or without crunch berries?"

She wrinkled her nose. "Gross. Granola, with raisins."

He shook his head. "That's it. Wedding is called off." He splashed as he walked, wetting her calves. "On to more serious matters. Name of your first grade teacher."

The questions went on way beyond twenty. The sun was setting over their left shoulders on the bay before they finally turned around and headed south toward the hotel again. Elise couldn't stop laughing, not just at some of Zane's crazy answers, but the way he said things. He was so genuinely confident in himself. So self-assured. So *real*. As they walked back up the beach toward the hotel and their shoes, Zane caught her arm to help her through the soft sand. "I'm starving. Those quarter-size hors d'oeuvres just didn't do anything for me." He looked to her. "You want to grab a burger before I take you home, Ellie?"

Ellie. He called her Ellie again. She liked it. She liked the way she felt when he called her that. "A burger would be good. Of course it will have be that dive now." She pointed to their abandoned shoes.

"There's no way I can wrestle into those hose again."

He laughed as he grabbed her shoes and passed them to her. "My car's just up the hill." They took a set of steps to the parking lot as he explained to her the finer points of grilling a good hamburger. He led her toward a vintage green BMW and opened the passenger door for her.

A gentleman *and* driving a BMW? The man was in the triple bonus round....

Elise tossed her sandy panty hose into the hamper. "She shoots, she scores!" she announced jubilantly.

She laughed. Shooting baskets with dirty hose? Talking out loud to herself? She didn't know what had gotten into her.

Yes, she did. Zane Keaton.

Dressed in sleek, satin pajamas, Elise padded barefoot down the hall to the spare bedroom she used as an office. She flipped a wall switch and soft light flooded the room painted in beige neutrals. From the desk, she grabbed a light blue piece of paper and a pen. She leaned over and wrote "Zane Keaton" in loopy handwriting on the top line of the *Husband Finder* checklist. She tucked a lock of her blond hair behind one ear and began to fill in Zane's physical details: 6'1", blond hair, blue eyes. She knew the worksheet was really for "official" dates, but "official" or not, her evening with Zane was the best date she had ever had. Well, maybe with the exception of

the hot Texas evening she'd spent with Johnny Car-
lisle when a traveling carnival had passed through
town, and she'd slipped out of the house. Of course
she'd only been fifteen at the time, and Johnny had
been her first kiss, so that probably didn't count.

Elise grabbed the paper and pen and took them
down the hall. She glanced at the Career heading and
halted in the middle of the living room.

She couldn't believe she hadn't asked Zane what
he did for a living. She'd spent an entire evening with
the man. He was such a good listener for a man. The
hours had slipped by like the seconds it took to enjoy
a bite-size candy bar. And she hadn't asked him about
his work. Her father would be horrified.

Elise held the pen poised over the Career section:
Professional, Business Owner, Other. She decided on
"other" just so she didn't have to leave the line
blank. She hated blank lines and the way they stared
accusingly at you. After all, what did it matter what
he did for a living? Zane was obviously going to score
high enough to warrant another date.

The phone rang and she glanced at the Irish por-
celain clock on an end table. It was almost midnight.
Eleven in Texas, too late for her father to call; he was
an early riser. She darted for the phone. Liz had said
she would call, to see how her evening went with
Zane. Elise was dying to tell her friend what a wonderful evening she'd had. To tell her about the barefoot walk and the fact that Zane had convinced her
to eat not just a burger, but fries, too. She had prob-

ably consumed an entire day's worth of calories in one sitting and she didn't care.

"Liz," she said excitedly into the phone.

"Ellie?"

The male voice startled her....

He'd called her Ellie.

"Zane?"

He chuckled, his voice low and sexy. "I didn't think you'd be in bed yet."

She glanced at the clock again. She'd barely been home half an hour. He had to have walked into his house and immediately picked up the phone to call her.

She didn't know what to say. The men she dated were never in a hurry to talk to her. They didn't call half an hour after they dropped her off—sometimes they never called again.

"No, no, it's fine," she said, settling on the pale green damask couch. She smoothed the protective arm cover. The piece of furniture was so expensive, a gift from her father, that she barely sat on it. She preferred the old leather recliner that she'd brought from home and kept in her office in the back. She'd had the recliner in her dorm room at college, then her very first apartment. She liked the smell of the old leather.

"I was just—" She looked down at the sheet of paper on the end table and felt a stab of guilt. "Just picking up a little before I went to bed," she lied cheerfully.

"Well, I wanted to tell you that I enjoyed my evening with you."

"Well, I did, too."

"So, I was wondering."

She held her breath. She didn't care what the book said about not relying on chemistry. Right now, it felt too darned good.

"Think we could get together later this week?"

"Sure," she said trying not to sound overly eager.

"I thought I could tell you what I was looking for in the way of property, and you could look into what's available."

If her stomach could have literally dropped, it would have been on the floor. *He wanted to talk about property?* "Um, sure, that would be great."

"I've got a lot going this week, but how about Friday?"

"Friday is good."

"I'll call you later in the week."

"Sounds good," she said, trying to sound equally cheery.

"'Night, Ellie," Zane said in that same sexy voice that made her feel warm all over.

"'Night, Zane."

Elise barely hung up the cordless phone when it rang again. This time it had to be Liz.

"That you, Liz?"

"Expecting Leonardo or Brad so late?" Liz's voice was laced with her usual blend of amusement and sarcasm.

Elise curled up on the couch, tucking her bare feet beneath her. "You're never going to believe what an evening I've had," she said not knowing if she wanted to laugh or cry.

"That good?"

"Well, I think so. Zane just called and said he wanted to get together later in the week."

"That's wonderful!" Liz exclaimed.

"To talk about real estate."

"Oh." Liz's voice fell.

"But I really like him," Elise said softly. "And he's already met several of the criteria."

"So meet him. Talk to him about some property. Let him get to know you. Business luncheons will turn into romantic interludes before you know it. It happens all the time."

Elise smiled. "Thanks, Liz. See you Monday."

Chapter Two

Don't be fooled by fairy tales; frogs do not turn into princes. Appearances can mean everything to the contemporary working woman. We are judged by what we drive and where we live.

"Hey, Pops! How are you this morning?" Zane leaned over and kissed the top of his grandfather's bald head. "Look who I brought."

Zane's black Lab, Scootie, wagged his tail, sending his whole backside swinging and licked Tom Keaton's wrinkled hands, folded neatly in his lap the way his nurse had left them.

The old man smiled vaguely and patted the dog's head when Scootie rested his snout on Tom's bony knee.

"I thought we'd go for a walk outside, Pops. How would that be?" Zane studied his grandfather's face for some response, any response. There was none. "Great," Zane said. "Here we go!" He unlocked the brake on his grandfather's wheelchair and wheeled him out of the "Family Room" of the Alzheimer's wing.

"Taking Pops for a walk, Katie," Zane called cheerfully as he passed the nurse's station.

"I'll buzz you out," the cute blonde answered. "Have a nice walk."

"We always do." With the dog trailing behind him, he pushed the wheelchair through the set of double doors that were locked to keep the patients inside. His grandfather wore a band on his wrist as an extra safety precaution. The wristband set off an alarm any time he passed through the doors of the ward. The band helped to alert the staff if he wandered away on those days when he could still walk on his own.

"I went to that benefit dinner for the hospital last night, Pops." Zane pushed the wheelchair down the hallway, headed for the doors that exited into the garden area. "I gave Mr. Johann your check and told him how disappointed you were that you couldn't be there yourself. And guess what else happened?" He hit a big silver pad on the wall and the doors swung open, allowing him to push the wheelchair through. Scootie burst through the door first, into the morning sunshine.

"I met a girl. You'd like her. She's cute and she's funny and she's smart."

The doors swung closed behind them.

"I really liked her," he said thoughtfully, shaking his head. "She's a real estate agent. A real go-getter according to Richard."

Zane pushed his grandfather around a small circular herb garden, headed for the tomato patch. Tom Keaton had always grown some of the best tomatoes in Sussex County, and the hospital had been nice enough to give him a small flower bed to plant. Other patients would come out and pick them when they were ripe; Tom just liked to see the plants.

"You know how I feel about women like that, Pops. They just aren't for me. They don't care about anything but their job. No family ties. No purpose in life except work twelve hour days and make money. I'm looking for a woman who wants to be a part of my life the way grandma was a part of your life."

Zane's mother had been one of those women who put her career ahead of her family. She'd been so wrapped up in her advertising job that she'd never had time for him and his sister. She'd missed the only home run he ever hit playing Little League baseball, when he was ten. She'd never attended his band concerts. Never brought homemade cupcakes to school for his birthday like the other moms. His parents had finally divorced when he was twelve, and she now lived in New York City, working for a big shot ad company. He rarely saw her, and when he did, they were casual strangers.

"As soon as I found out what Ellie—that's her name—what Ellie did for a living, I know I shouldn't have asked her out, but I did." He grabbed a stick and hurled it in the air. Scootie took off after it. "Well, sort of."

He chuckled as he pushed the wheelchair up close to the small patch of tomato plants and plucked a weed that had sneaked up through the mulch. "I couldn't help myself. She was just so nice and fun to be with."

He looked down at his grandfather who stared at the plants. "And it wasn't *really* a date I asked her out on anyway. I told her I was looking for land to buy. And that's kind of true. I mean we're always looking for good farmland, right?"

He paused. "I know. Even that's a mistake. I'm just setting myself up for another fall. I can just see the whole thing with Judy happening all over again. One call and off she goes to Singapore for a job promotion. So much for the engagement ring. So much for good ol' Zane."

He crouched down beside the wheelchair and scooped up a little dirt. He pressed it into his grandfather's hand and closed the old man's fingers around it.

Somewhere in Tom's clouded, pale blue eyes, Zane sensed some kind of recognition. Zane lifted his grandfather's feeble hand close to his nose so that he could breathe in the scent of the warm, dark soil.

"The thing is, Pops, I *really* liked her. I was thinking about taking her out in the boat on Friday. Showing her your dad's land. What do you think?"

Zane carefully loosened his grandfather's hands and sprinkled the dirt onto the ground again. "I know, do what I think's best. You'll always support me."

He sighed and sat back on the bench. Scootie dropped the stick at his feet and Zane threw it as far as he could. The dog bounded off and to Zane's delight, his grandfather smiled.

"You like it when I bring Scootie, don't you?" Zane leaned forward. "Here, let me get that." He pulled a handkerchief from the breast pocket of his grandfather's plaid shirt and gently wiped the old man's mouth. He refolded it and tucked it back into the pocket, giving it a pat.

As if on cue, the black Lab came bounding back, stick in his mouth and he collapsed at the foot of the wheelchair.

"Hey, look who's back, Pops!" Zane gave Scootie a scratch between the ears. "So how about a walk down the path, through the woods?" he asked, already on his feet, grabbing the wheelchair.

"Here we go." He pushed his grandfather down the walk. The dog bounded past them, familiar with the path they took several days a week. "Think we can take him if we run?"

"Yeah, I think so, too," Zane answered for Tom. And then he took off at a run, pushing the wheelchair.

Grandfather opened his arms and tipped back his head and grinned, enjoying the feel of the breeze on his face.

To Zane, that smile was worth a million dollars.

Wednesday morning, Elise headed downtown in her car to drop off some paperwork for a client. She hadn't heard from Zane yet, but she guessed he would call her tonight. She had a women's business league meeting right after work, but she'd skip the dinner afterward, just to be sure she was home when he called. She was trying hard not to get her hopes up. He hadn't said he wanted a date. He'd said he wanted to talk about real estate.

Elise signaled and turned left onto a divided road that went through the middle of town. As she passed an old beat-up pickup truck, out of the corner of her eye, she caught a glimpse of a familiar face.

It couldn't be.

She slowed down so that the dilapidated truck passed her in the right lane. The truck spat and sputtered as it chugged along, bits of straw blowing out of its bed. It didn't even have a typical Delaware state license plate, but instead had a tag, that read Farm Vehicle in black block letters. The body of the truck was blue. Rusted blue. The original tailgate had been replaced sometime when she was a teenager with a red one. The tailgate's rust matched the body's quite nicely.

Elise clutched the steering wheel of her imported sedan as the driver came into view again. He had the radio blasting to some old rock station that played hits from the seventies and eighties. The song "Ballroom Blitz" blared and he sang along. His dusty ball cap was pulled down low over his brow, one muscular, tanned arm rested on the open window as he tapped to the tune.

The farmer looked like Zane.

It couldn't be Zane, of course. Zane drove a BMW sedan. Even though she didn't know what he did for a living, she could guess from the kind of man he was. She was certain he was working in an office somewhere right now. Wearing a gray business suit, ordering employees around. At the very least he was having lunch with a client, sipping a nice wine and ordering Caesar salad with the dressing on the side.

They say everyone has a twin, she told herself, trying not to hyperventilate as she let the truck pull away from her. She ignored the guy in the white car behind her who was tailgating in an effort to get her to speed up.

That farmer was obviously Zane's twin. Wasn't that a funny coincidence? Right here in their own town of Nassateague Bay.

Or maybe Zane had an identical twin brother and he just hadn't mentioned it. Maybe the farmer was a twin brother, that was it. A black sheep of the family.

Never made it to college. Worked on a potato farm. Planted and harvested soybeans for a living.

Elise forced herself to loosen her grip on the steering wheel and take a deep breath. She put down the passenger side window so she could get some air.

The tailgater passed her. "It's the pedal on the right," he shouted as he whizzed by.

Elise slowly pressed the accelerator until she was once again doing the speed limit. The pickup turned right at the next intersection. Without thinking, she signaled and switched lanes quickly so that she could follow the imposter.

It wasn't Zane. She knew the farmer wasn't Zane. He couldn't be Zane. There was no place to indicate "farmer" on *The Husband Finder* checklist. She had clearly stated in the career category that she was looking for a professional, a man who would understand her devotion to her profession. She tried not to panic as she followed the truck down a narrow side street.

Two blocks down, the truck made another right. She continued to follow at a safe distance.

The farmer wasn't Zane, and she was going to prove it to herself.

The truck pulled into a gravel parking lot. She had never been on this side of town. A sign on the side of the tin-roofed cement block building read Smitty's Seed & Feed. It was a feed store, for heaven's sake. A store where farmers bought their...animal provisions and bird seed, she supposed.

She slowed down, watching as the old truck

lurched to a halt and the door swung open. As she drove by, she saw the farmer lift his head, raise a hand and call good-naturedly to a man standing in an open door on the loading dock.

She knew that voice.

She knew that bad-boy blond hair sticking out from beneath the ball cap.

Elise drove by the store and kept going.

She was afraid she might cry.

A farmer? Zane farmed for a living? Now what? Career was a big heading on *The Husband Finder* checklist. It was even printed in bold. She'd already ignored the whole chemistry advice. Could she scratch out the career part, too? Would the list still work?

Elise pulled into a parking spot in front of her client's business and picked up her cell phone to call Liz's extension at work.

"Liz Jefferson."

"Liz," Elise said, feeling a little silly for even calling about this in the middle of the day. Liz was busy; personal lives were supposed to stay out of the office.

"Elise?"

"You're not going to believe this," Elise said. "I just saw Zane in town."

"And he canceled your date? Excuse me, your nondate?" she corrected. "Jerk."

"No, no. I didn't speak to him. I just saw him drive by."

"And he had a woman with him and a baby in a car seat in the back. The man's married. Jerk."

"No, Liz, listen to me. I saw Zane and he…he was driving a pickup. An *old* pickup." She took a deep breath. "Liz, he got out of the truck at a feed store wearing overalls."

"Sweet Mary, mother of Joseph," Liz swore.

"I don't think he's a doctor or a lawyer," Elise said. "What do I do?"

"What do you do?" Liz shrieked. "You cancel the date, of course. You were the top seller for Waterfront Realty last month. You don't date farmers."

Elise gathered her client's paperwork from the passenger's seat. She should have known that's what Liz would say. Liz was all about how things appeared. She didn't even date men who were junior partners in a firm. "You think?" Elise said in a small voice.

"Look at the book, peruse the checklist," Liz said firmly. "It's not one of the choices, sweetie. I don't care how fine-looking the man is."

"I have to go," Elise told Liz. "I'm dropping off Joe Carmine's contracts on that warehouse."

"Call and cancel the date," Liz insisted. "Just call, and leave a message on Zane's answering machine and tell him you can't meet him, but if he wants to talk about land, he can call the office and you'll be happy to see him."

"Gotta go, Liz," Elise said. "Talk to you later."

Elise climbed out of her car and delivered her client's contracts. Half an hour later, back in the car, she picked up her cell phone and stared at it. Was Liz right? Should she cancel now before things went any further with Zane? Just leave a message on his answering machine? He wasn't fitting the profile she'd laid out for herself. He wasn't the kind of man she wanted for a husband. Her whole attraction, so far, had been based on sheer chemistry. Right?

It was the right thing to do. Before she changed her mind, she hit the buttons on the phone, rehearsing what she would say as she waited for his answering machine to pick up.

Did farmers even have answering machines?

"Hello."

Zane's voice startled Elise so badly that she almost hung up. He was there? How was he there? She had just seen him at the feed store. Shouldn't he be out riding a tractor or something?

"Hello?" Zane repeated.

"Z-Zane," Elise said, trying to find her voice.

"Ellie."

She could almost hear his smile over the phone. "Yes, it's Elise." She paused. She knew what she needed to say now. She needed to tell him that she couldn't make it Friday night. That was all she had to say. She didn't need to make an excuse. In business, one never made excuses.

"Hey, you're not calling to bail out on me, are you?" he asked suspiciously.

"N-no, no of course not." The words just tumbled out of her mouth before she could stop them.

He had called her Ellie. He had smiled when he said her name. He was so darned *nice.*

She took a deep breath. Why was she listening to other people instead of herself? The heck with Liz. The heck with her father's voice in her head. Maybe she'd just made a mistake when she'd filled out the career part in *The Husband Finder.* Maybe she was supposed to be more general. "Of course I'm not canceling," she said.

"Well, good, because I'm really looking forward to seeing you. I've been thinking about you all week."

"You have?" she said softly.

"Mmm-hmm. I actually turned down my sister's garlic roast for you. She called last night to see if I wanted to come to dinner Friday night, and I told her I was busy."

That was so sweet. No man had ever turned down his sister's roast for her before.

"So," she said. "What are you doing home this time of day? I...I thought I would get your answering machine. I was...just calling to see what I should wear Friday. You said you wanted to talk about some land, but I didn't know if that meant drinks... dinner?" she said, hoping she didn't come on too strong.

"Dress casual. Wear sneakers. No panty hose. I want to take you out on my boat, show you a piece of land I'm interested in. As for why I'm home, I'm here because I wanted to check my chicks before I went by the office.''

What he said about the boat went right over her head. She heard the word *office* and her heart buoyed. She didn't know what the deal with the old truck and the overalls was, but he worked in an office. Farmers didn't have offices.

Then she realized he had said "chicks." Surely he didn't run a topless dancing place or something. "Your chicks?" she asked.

He laughed. "Baby chicks. Peeps. You know. *Gallus domesticus*. Chickens. As in Kentucky Fried. I raise chickens.''

A chicken farmer? Her prince who was going to save her from a life of microwave popcorn dinners and lonely nights with Letterman was a chicken farmer? There was no way chicken farmer was going to fit on that itty bitty line on *The Husband Finder* checklist.

"Chickens?" she managed. "You raise chickens?''

"Actually eggs. These chicks are a new breed I'm trying out. I like to keep my eye on them myself. So how's six?''

"Six? Six is good." Elise felt numb to the tips of her toes and she didn't think it was because her shoes were too tight. "I'll be ready at six. I...I'll meet you at the boat dock. I'll have to come right from work.''

He gave her directions to the place on the bay

where he put out his boat. Elise just kept nodding like a numb wit.

"Listen, I'd better get back to work," Zane said.

"Me, too," Elise answered, as if coming out of her daze.

"See you Friday on the dock?"

"See you Friday."

She hung up and sat there in her car for a moment staring at the cell phone in her hand. A smile found its way to her face as she was filled with a strange sense of confidence. A chicken farmer? So what if he was a chicken farmer? He was still the finest looking chicken farmer *she'd* ever seen in a tux.

He was the only chicken farmer she'd ever seen in a tux.

She'd just squeeze it in on the checklist.

Smiling to himself, Zane hung up the phone on the wall by the refrigerator. He was looking forward to seeing Ellie on Friday; he was glad he had set aside his concerns about her occupation.

He opened the refrigerator and poured himself a glass of lemonade. Elise Montgomery wasn't the kind of woman Zane usually dated. He tended to go for the earthy sort; flowered skirts, long, flowing hair, recycling fanatics. Kindergarten teachers. Social workers. He wished he'd asked Ellie more about her work. She had told him that she worked for a realty company. He wondered if selling real estate was just a job to her or if she was a "career woman." He hadn't had much luck with career women. In fact, he'd made a pact with himself to stay away from them.

First there had been his mother; she'd never been meant to have a husband, children. Then he'd dated Judy, one of his researchers for two years, and then asked her to marry him. They had actually been looking at wedding dates when she'd gotten the chance to take a job in Singapore. She had told Zane that she had deep feelings for him, but that she was at a point in her life when she had to put herself and her career first. As much as he hated to admit it, then and now, Judy had really hurt him. Now, as uncool and as backward as it sounded, he was looking for a woman ready to devote herself to a relationship. He wanted a woman to be able to devote her life to him the way he wanted to devote his life to someone he loved.

Zane finished off his lemonade and set the glass in the sink. He pushed open the screen door and crossed the back porch of the farmhouse he had grown up in. His father and his grandparents had made it a warm, welcoming home, and it was his hope that some day he would raise a family here.

Of course, first, he needed a wife. And he didn't need a wife whose job was more important than her family. So far, the wife hunting wasn't going so well. He was tired of casual dating however, the women he'd met just didn't light his fire. But Ellie, there was something about Ellie that was different than all the others.

Her designer dresses and nice shoes somehow didn't quite ring true. Didn't quite fit. There was something innocent about her, despite her worldliness. In his mind's eye he could see curling up by the fireplace in the front room with her in the evening, cuddled under one of Grandma's quilts, sharing their day with each other. He could see making babies with her in the four-poster bed he now slept in alone. He could imagine sharing his dreams with her…his life.

Was he crazy? Richard had stood there at the hospital dinner and said Elise Montgomery was a high-powered broker. He might as well have looked right at Zane and said "This woman isn't for you."

But Zane really liked her. And their date really wasn't a date anyway, was it? He'd just have to keep that in mind on Friday.

Chapter Three

Beware of sentimentalities. Stick with concrete facts when assessing your man. The contemporary woman of today doesn't have time for trivial overromanticizing.

Elise waited nervously in the front seat of her car, glancing at the boat dock every few minutes. She was early. Zane said six o'clock, but she'd left work at five to run to the store.

Unable to suppress her delight, she glanced down at the bright white tennis shoes she was wearing. She'd been able to find an ancient pair of jean shorts and an old T-shirt in the bottom of her closet, but she'd been at a loss as to what to wear on her feet for this date. She had running shoes, racquetball sneakers and cross-trainers, but nothing suitable to wear on a boat.

On impulse, after work, Elise had stopped at the dollar store near the office and bought a pair of plain white tennis shoes. Only five dollars. She'd never been in a dollar store in her life and had enjoyed herself thoroughly. She'd come out not just with the tennis shoes, but a set of hot mitts, a refrigerator magnet and a box of Post-Its. The grand total of her purchases had been eight dollars. She hadn't realized having fun could be so cheap.

Elise glanced up at the sound of tires on gravel and saw the now familiar Ford pickup pulling a boat that, like the truck, had seen better days. Zane waved out the window. Well, it was more like a salute.

Elise didn't usually date men who waved or saluted out windows.

Delighted, she waved back. He didn't *act* like a man who just wanted to talk about real estate.

Zane pulled the truck around and began to back the boat down the ramp into the water. Elise grabbed her cell phone and her purse, but as she locked the door, she hesitated. What did she need her purse for? They would be out in the bay. She popped her trunk with her key fob and tossed her purse in. She hesitated with the phone. She never went anywhere without the phone. What if her boss needed her? Or a client? "You don't need it," Zane hollered across the parking lot, seeming to know just what she was thinking. "Ringing phones scare away the crabs!"

She looked at him suspiciously. She knew nothing about crabbing. "They do?"

"They scare me away." He grinned again.

"What the heck. Live on the wild side," Elise muttered to herself. There had been nothing in the book about that. In fact, it had suggested a woman needed to find a man who would fit into *her* comfort zone. She tossed the phone into the trunk and tucked her keys into her jean shorts pocket.

"What can I do to help?" She crossed the parking lot.

He climbed into the boat, using the trailer's wheel well as a step. "Grab the cooler out of the back of the truck—the canvas bag, too."

At the rear of the truck, she peered over the side. There were two burlap bags of some sort of feed, a large bag that read Oyster Shells on the side, a cooler, a canvas tote bag and lots of loose straw. She picked up the blue cooler and the bag and carried them to the side of the boat.

"Once I get her in the water, I'll need you to hold the mooring line while I park the truck."

She handed up the cooler and the bag. "You sure this thing is seaworthy?" She lifted an eyebrow as she studied the boat.

The boat was about twenty-two feet long, white with a wood interior that was definitely not teak. Plywood? There were no holes in its hull, but the boat had obviously been used for many years. Elise had never been in a little motorboat before, just big sailboats, and a few yachts in her days in Texas.

Zane slapped the side of the boat. "Old *Betsy*'s seaworthy all right and she knows where the crabs hide."

"Betsy?"

"The boat was my dad's. Named after some old girlfriend, or something."

He jumped out of the boat to the ground and wiped his hands on the back pockets of a pair of old khaki shorts. "Okay, now I'm going to lower her in. See that line on the bow?"

He walked to the front of the boat and began to crank on a turn handle. Elise spotted the rope, but she was nervous about the idea of holding the boat on her own. The boats she had been on before had deckhands for this kind of stuff.

"Just grab it," he instructed.

He gave a wave when she didn't hop to it right away. The boat was halfway off the trailer and easing into the water. "It won't really be heavy. She'll swing around along the dock there. You just have to hold her a sec."

Elise reached up and grabbed the rope, determined to be a good sport.

He continued to crank on the winch, the muscles of his upper arms flexing as he turned the handle. Nice biceps. Through his thin navy T-shirt she could see he had nice pecs, too.

The bow of the boat hit the water with a splash and Elise tightened her grip on the mooring line. Zane balanced on one of the metal supports of the trailer and walked out to the end to unhook the winch line from the bow. "Be right back."

He parked the truck and trailer and was at her side in no time, taking the line. "Jump in and we're off."

Elise didn't know whether the tide was coming in or out, but the floor of the boat was a good three feet below the dock.

He grabbed her hand. "Just step onto the cushion on the bench and you're in."

His touch was warm. Powerful. It sent tingles of pleasure down her spine. Feeling silly at her reaction, she gripped Zane's hand and stepped gingerly into the boat. This wasn't high school. There was no need to get all weak in the knees over a simple brush of this guy's hand. The book had warned her that these feelings would get her nowhere.

He climbed in behind her, tossed the rope onto the bow and grabbed a net off the floor. Using the wooden handle, he pushed off from the dock.

"You swim?" He straddled the captain's seat in front of the steering wheel.

Elise took a bench seat that ran along the side of the boat. "Swim team in high school. State champ in the butterfly."

"Okay, so you swim better than I do." He grinned. "Anyway, there are plenty of life jackets under the bench you're sitting on." He turned a key and the outboard motor started to rumble. "Ready?"

She nodded. "Ready."

They were soon cutting across the bay. Elise hadn't thought she would enjoy the motorboat ride. Wind in her face, salt spray in her hair. But it was a beautiful evening. As they drove along the shore, Zane pointed out long-legged seabirds and a school of shimmering fish. Seagulls flew overhead and a blue heron soared by. The air smelled of salt water and sunshine and a kind of happiness she hadn't felt in a long time.

They didn't talk as the boat cut across the bay. The motor was too noisy and Elise was too caught up in the moment. She didn't care if there wasn't a place on her husband finder for a crabbing date, she was glad she had come. There was something about the simplicity of the outing, the simplicity of Zane that held her spellbound.

After fifteen or twenty minutes Zane eased the boat near to the shore and cut the engine. He climbed up over the windshield and tossed an anchor.

"There it is." He pointed to the shore.

She gazed out over the water at the property he pointed to. "I've heard through the grapevine that the owner might possibly want to sell. I've approached him several times, but he wouldn't talk to me. He has some beef with my family over a crate of chickens or something silly like that from back in the forties. Maybe you could do something?" He looked up hopefully.

She studied the point of land. All she could see was marsh grass that led to a pine woods. "What's beyond there?" she asked.

"Used to be fields, now it's mostly overgrown meadows. My grandfather grew up on that land. His father lost it during the Depression. He used to take me out here in his boat and show it to me. I've always thought I'd like to buy it back for him."

He gave a little smile and once again she thought about how good-hearted he was. Why hadn't there been a place on the checklist for good-hearted?

He clapped his hands together. "So. Ready to catch some crabs?"

"Ah, I don't know. I really just came for the ride, you know to see which property you were talking about," she stalled. "You can crab and I can watch." Truthfully, she wanted to try it, but she wasn't used to not knowing how to do something. Out here on the bay, she felt as if she was totally out of her element.

"Cut me a break, real estate woman. It's easy. Once you catch your first jimmy, you'll be hooked." He lifted the seat of the bench across from the one she was sitting on and tossed her something.

Elise instinctively threw up both hands and caught the object. It was wet and slimy. "Ewww." She looked at the thing in her hand wrapped with a string and some metal bolts.

"Chicken neck," he explained. "Bait. Blue claws love them."

Elise didn't know what to do. She wanted to drop

the icky thing. But suddenly she wanted to crab even more.

"Just tie it on and drop the neck overboard. The bolts serve as weight to keep the line from swaying too much with the outgoing tide."

Chicken. It was just chicken. After watching him throw one of the necks over the side and grab another one, she unwound the string and leaned over the side of the boat. "You sure this is going to work? I thought people crabbed with crab pots."

"Lazy man's crabbing." He threw back his shoulders. "That's okay if you make your living crabbing, but I'm purist." He tossed another line over the side of the boat and tied the other end to a small bracket on the wall of the boat. "Want another?"

"Nah. One's good." She stared at the string she had unwound in one hand, the chicken in the other. "Now how do I do this?"

He crossed from one side of the boat to the other cautiously and sat down next to her. As he reached for her string, his bare knee brushed hers. There they were again, those tingles of pleasure.

His gaze met hers and lingered for just a second. She knew he had felt it, too.

He blinked and looked down. "Just tie it in a knot like this," he explained as he did it for her.

She watched his hands as he wrapped the string. They were nice hands. Clean. Capable.

Sexy.

For a second she imagined what it would be like

to feel those hands caress her cheek. Elsewhere. Somehow she knew he would instinctively know just how to touch her. Maybe it was that good heart.

"Then toss it over."

His words startled her, bringing her back to reality.

He dropped it into the water, got up and went back to his seat. Which was just as well. Elise couldn't seem to think clearly with him so close.

She glanced into the dark water that lapped against the side of the boat. She couldn't see a thing. "Now what?"

"Now we wait." He sat on the bench facing her. "We wait and we eat." He reached for the cooler.

Elise and Zane shared a dinner of grocery store fried chicken, deli potato salad, raw carrots and dip and grapes for dessert. Not a bad meal coming from a single man. He'd actually included a vegetable that truly was a veggie and not another carb. To drink, he'd brought along homemade iced tea in a thermos.

Twice while they were eating they stopped to check their lines. Just as Elise was finishing her second drumstick, Zane waved to her with one hand. "Get the net."

Elise jumped up so quickly that she rocked the boat. "Whoa."

Zane grabbed her around her waist with one hand and they swayed together, hip pressed against hip. Slowly the boat grew still again.

"You okay?" he said quietly. His mouth was inches from hers.

And a great mouth it was. Well shaped. Sensual.

The boat had ceased rocking, but she was feeling a little unsteady on her feet. It was his nearness. The faint scent of his cologne. It had never occurred to her that chicken farmers might wear expensive cologne.

"I'm okay," she said, stepping back, her gaze still locked on his.

"Think we should get that crab?" he murmured, catching her ogling again. Fortunately, his tone was playful.

"Umm. Sure." Elise laughed as she passed him the net and knelt beside him on the bench to peer into the murky water. He slowly inched up the crab line, bringing the chicken neck closer to the surface. Sure enough, he had a crab.

"I see it," Elise said excitedly.

Zane swung the net and scooped the blue claw crab out of the water.

"You think I have one?" she asked, crossing to her own side of the boat. She knelt and grabbed the line, pulling it up the way she had seen Zane do it. "I've got one, I've got one," she cried, waving her hand.

"Want the net?" Zane dumped his crab into the bushel basket he had brought along for that purpose.

"You do it," she said. "I'm afraid it will get away."

Zane swung the net in his experienced hand and scooped up her crab.

"I can't believe I got one." She pulled the neck and line out of the net. "Maybe I can get another." As she dropped the line over the side of the boat again, she put out her hand. "I think you're right, I'm going to need another line."

He laughed. "Coming up."

The sun was just setting over the bay as Elise and Zane motored back to the dock. She helped him bring the boat out of the water and repack everything in the bed of his truck including three quarters of a bushel of crabs.

"I can't believe we got so many," she said as she helped him tighten the straps that secured the boat to the trailer.

"Now you have to come help eat them. Crab feast tomorrow, my place at one o'clock sharp."

She clutched her hands. She smelled like bay water and crab. Her shorts were damp and her hair was a mess. The best part was that she didn't care. "I…I don't know. I usually work Saturday afternoons."

"You can't catch crabs and not eat them. It's a felony." He stood in front of her, both hands planted on his hips. "Please tell me you eat crabs. Because if you don't, it's goodbye right here and now," he teased. "I'll take my crabs and my business elsewhere."

She laughed. "Okay. I am originally from Texas, but I've been an East Coaster for years. I eat crabs."

"And you pick your own?"

She laughed again. "I pick my own. Had a college roommate who showed me how."

He walked her back to her car. "Then I'll see you tomorrow. No ifs, ands, or buts. I'll call my sister and my cousins—see if they want to come, too."

She leaned against the hood of her car. His family? Family gatherings terrified her. Back in Texas whenever there was a family gathering it had usually involved martinis, shouting and breaking glass. Besides, she wasn't quite sure what was going on between them. When he called, he had made it sound like he just wanted to show her the property he was interested in buying. This was now looking more like a date every minute. And crabs at his place definitely sounded like a date…almost. She hesitated. "I don't know."

"Oh, come on. You'll like them," he assured her, coming to stand right in front of her. "My sister and cousins are great. And my cousin Mattie has the sweetest little girl, Olivia. She's only four, but she's really smart."

He was grinning. She couldn't resist smiling back.

He put one hand on each side of her hips, leaning closer. "I'm glad you came, Ellie. I mean, I'm glad I got to show you that property." For a man who seemed so sure of himself, he didn't seem so sure right now and it was utterly charming.

She couldn't take her gaze from his. He had the most beautiful blue eyes.

"You know," he said. "I realize you just came out

to see that property and that I didn't actually ask you out, but—''

She waited, almost tasting the anticipation of what he would say on the tip of her tongue.

''But I really want to kiss you,'' Zane confessed as he brushed his knuckles against her cheek, in a slow, deliberate, sexy manner.

''But you haven't *because…?*''

''I don't know.'' He lifted one shoulder. ''Chicken?''

She laughed as much at his honesty and his play on words, considering his occupation, but his husky voice made her tremble. She had never talked about kissing before. Not like this and certainly not with a potential *client*. It made her throat dry, her palms damp. Her gaze shifted to his lips. ''So what if a girl wants to be kissed?'' she whispered.

He leaned closer, not taking his gaze from hers. His mouth turned up in a movie-star smirk and he leaned closer. ''Then I guess I get up my gumption and I kiss her.''

Elise closed her eyes, lifting her chin, mesmerized by the scent of him, by his nearness. His arms tightened around her waist as his lips brushed hers, tentatively and then with more pressure. She slid her hands over his chest, around his neck as a spark seemed to literally leap between them. It was the best kiss she'd ever had in her life.

One that didn't last nearly long enough.

"Man, I shouldn't be doing this," Zane whispered still holding her in his arms.

She lifted her lashes to look at him. "What do you mean?" *Please don't let him be married,* she thought.

"Nothing." He sighed.

She made herself ask. "You're not married, right?"

He shook his head. "Never been married. Come close, but... Look, it's not you, Ellie. Really. It's me. Like I said before, long story." He took a step back, releasing her. "So you'll come to my place for crabs, right?"

She unlocked her car door, still dizzy from the euphoria of Zane's kiss. "I'll be there," she heard herself say. "The heck with work!"

The phone was ringing when Elise walked into her apartment. Could it be Zane again? "Hello?" she said, quickly dropping her purse on the counter.

"Elise Anne."

"Father." She couldn't resist a little sigh of disappointment. She was feeling so good right now that she hated to speak with him. Somehow he always had a way of making her feel small. Incompetent.

"I tried you at the office," he said. "You weren't in. Out showing property?"

"Umm...yes." She grabbed a bottle of water out of the refrigerator. It wasn't exactly a lie. "So how are you?"

"Busy. Preparing for our next shareholders' meeting. You know it's getting to be a lot for me. I was thinking tonight that if *you* were here," he said pointedly, "you could be helping me run the business as you should be. You could take some of the burden for me."

Not this again. It was like a broken record with him. "Father, I'm a real estate agent. I know nothing about the oil business."

"You know about hard work," he said gruffly. "How many times have you won top salesman of the month in your office this year?"

"Every time," she said quietly.

"Five months in a row," he grunted. "And when your sales numbers come in for June, I'll guarantee you it will be six. It's in the Montgomery blood. Hard work and self-sacrifice pays off."

She stared through the doorway of the kitchen into the living room at her beautiful carpet. Her beautiful furniture. Looking at it, knowing it was hers, didn't give her half the satisfaction she had gotten out of catching her own crabs tonight. She could sit on that damask couch a thousand times and it would never feel as good as Zane's single kiss.

"Umm. I have a little news," she said.

"Your employers have realized it's time they make you a partner?"

She kicked off her sneakers and walked through the living room, down the hall to her office. "I met a nice guy."

"I've told you before, Elise Anne. Waste of time,

dating these days. Monique and I just filed for divorce.''

Monique was her father's fourth wife. Elise had only met her once, at the wedding. She'd been a cold fish—perfect for her father. ''I'm sorry to hear that,'' she said. And she meant it. She felt sorry for her father because she knew he had to be lonely. He just didn't realize it.

''Thank God I had the good sense to see that prenup lawyer before the wedding. This won't be anything but a blip on the radar screen. Listen, I have to go. A call coming in from California.''

''Okay, well, thanks for calling,'' she said.

''Right.''

Her father hung up and she listened to the dial tone for a moment before she set the phone on her desk. She wondered what her father would have said if she had told him Zane was a chicken farmer.

Her gaze strayed from the phone on her desk to the *Husband Finder* checklist beside it. She picked it up, hesitated for a moment and then grabbed a bold magic marker. In a childish fit of retaliation against her father and all Edwin Montgomery stood for, she wrote beneath the Career heading, ''Chicken Farmer'' in daring block print. Then she scanned both sheets front and back.

There was no place to write ''good heart'' or ''sentimental.'' She could note the type of car Zane drove, how well he was invested in the stock market, how many times he had been divorced, but there was no place to say that he was a thirty-five-year-old man who wanted to buy back his grandfather's childhood farm so the family could own it once again. With her bold marker, she scrawled across top of the first page, *Good Heart. Ten point bonus!*

And then she smiled, feeling better about herself than she had in a very long time.

Chapter Four

It's imperative that a man and woman's life-styles mesh. Having similar upbringings lends itself to successful relationships and successful marriages.

The following day, Elise rose with a strange sense that her life was changing. She worked out at the gym in the morning, and then cleaned her apartment, giving it a good once-over. With her bathroom tile sparkling, she took a long soak in the tub and read a paperback novel someone had passed to her years ago. At twelve-thirty, she grabbed some marinated mushrooms, one of the few things she could make that were edible, and headed for Zane's. She never called into the office and she didn't check her voice mail. For once she wanted to forget about work. She just wanted to try being who she thought she might want to be. Her father, a seven-day-workweek work-aholic, would have had a cow if he'd known. It was probably the first Saturday she hadn't worked since she was sixteen and started her first job in her father's office filing paperwork.

And it felt incredible.

Elise followed Zane's directions on a meandering country road and turned down a long lane, not sure what to expect. The closest she had ever been to a chicken farm was the glossy photos of one she had sold last year and that buyer had purchased it sight unseen. All she knew about chicken farms was that they consisted of long row houses that she saw dotting the countryside and that they were big business in the county.

She pulled her car into the yard under a big oak tree beside Zane's old pickup and some other cars including the BMW sedan he had taken her home in that night. She stared in awe at the white clapboard farmhouse with its wraparound screen porch and green shutters. The property was as neat as a pin with a freshly mowed lawn and trimmed hedges. It looked like it had come right out of a Disney movie, down to the tire swing hanging from a shade tree in the backyard.

Taking a deep breath, Elise climbed out of her car, hugging her Tupperware container of marinated mushrooms and cut across the lawn toward the house. A black Labrador retriever raced by her, carrying a small white sneaker, shortly followed by identical twin boys of seven or eight. They squealed with delight as they blew by her, one boy hopping along in his stocking foot as he tried to chase down his shoe.

Elise heard a screen door slap shut, and she looked up to see Zane strolling toward her, drying his hands on a towel. He was dressed in a pair of navy shorts and a surfing T-shirt, his boyish blond hair brushed casually to one side. He looked good. Young. More like a surfer than a chicken farmer this afternoon. "You made it," he called.

She nodded, feeling a little flustered at seeing him again. A day later, she could still taste his mouth on hers. Still feel his hands on her hips. And then there was that yearning in her belly. "I made it. I brought marinated mushrooms." She offered them. "I don't know if they go with crabs, but it's one of the few things I can make that isn't toxic."

"Not much of a cook, huh?" he asked.

She shook her head. "Not much."

He studied her for a moment as if processing that information. "Well," he said. "Luckily my sister makes a mean potato salad. Come on up on the porch. Crabs are steaming and just about ready to eat. I'll tell you who's who in this crazy family of mine."

She followed him.

"The dog that just ran by is my best buddy, Scootie. That's Meagan, my sister, on the porch with her new baby girl, Alyssa. She's got three more rug rats, all boys, around here somewhere. We don't bother with their names half the time—we use numbers. Her husband is Ted in charge of the crab steamer around back. Big guy.'' He drew his hands across his chest. ''State cop.'' He opened the door for her. ''That's my cousin Mattie with the red hair, and her daughter Olivia. She's the one I was telling you about.'' He pointed to a young woman in her early thirties with a little girl on her lap. ''Her twin boys, Noah and Zeb, are the ones running around the house screaming like wild things. Mattie's husband Joe and my other cousin, Carter, will be back soon. Carter's getting married soon—his fiancée, Amy, couldn't make it. The guys went out for beer. Apparently my home-made iced tea doesn't suit them.''

She smiled feeling a little overwhelmed.

''Don't worry, there won't be a test.'' Zane stood on the brick step and held the screen door to the porch open for her. ''And that's my grandfather,'' he said quietly.

Elise's gaze settled on the elderly man seated in a wheelchair on the far side of the porch, near the picnic table that had been covered with newspaper. Someone had turned his chair around so that he could see the field beyond the grassy line of the backyard.

''He has Alzheimer's,'' Zane said explained. ''He lives in a home now—my dad and I just couldn't take care of him anymore.'' His gaze rested on his grand-father; Elise could hear the love in his voice. The pain. And her first impulse was to touch him in some way. She brushed her hand against his.

"We don't know what he understands anymore, what he doesn't. He gets very confused. Forgets how to brush his teeth, drink from a straw. Walk." Zane shrugged. "Some days he seems to be better than others. We talk to him like he knows what's going on anyway. You never know."

She walked up the steps, passing him.

"All, this is Elise," Zane called over the din of all his family members talking at once. Several looked at her with interest. "I'm not making introductions. You can do that yourself. Just be nice," he warned. He indicated the door to the house. "Want to help me inside for a sec?"

She smiled, relieved. She wasn't sure she was ready to be thrown to the family lions yet. "Sure."

The inside of the house was as quaint as the outside. There was a big eat-in kitchen with a table covered with a red-checked tablecloth. An airy living room with a fireplace that looked like you could burn wood in it...and a big-screen TV. She'd seen enough houses to know a man ruled this roost. There was also a den Zane used as an office and a full bathroom on the first floor. A large center staircase that she assumed led to bedrooms upstairs dominated the front hall.

Zane's house was nothing like the grand, hollow marble mansion she had grown up in. It wasn't like her apartment either, where there was never a thing out of place. A place that was cold and unwelcoming no matter what additional shades she added to the color palette of her rooms at the suggestion of her decorator. Zane's home was full of warmth and life. A homemade quilt thrown over a couch that looked more like a piece of artwork than a bedcovering. A pile of newspapers beside the chair in front of the TV. On the refrigerator, there was even children's artwork. A gift to Uncle Zane, no doubt, from one of his nieces or nephews.

At Zane's instruction, Elise helped him carry all the makings of a Delmarva crab feast onto the screened-in section of the back porch. Two picnic tables covered in newsprint were piled high with spicy steamed blue claws, buttery corn on the cob, homemade potato salad and fried chicken for those who didn't want to attempt the crabs.

For the next two hours, Elise sat beside Zane and listened to the family banter. In a way, it was mind-boggling. The noise. The confusion. The phone was ringing and the dog was barking. Babies were crying. Children ran out the back door, across the porch, around the house, in through the front door and back onto the porch again. There was lots of laughter and good-natured teasing. Zane's brother-in-law created a sculpture of empty beer cans on the end of the porch, and the children took turns bowling them over with apples they had taken off the kitchen table.

Elise was completely overwhelmed by the melee, and fascinated at the very same time. Everyone was so nice to each other. There were no fights and no cold shoulders. No one threatened to remove anyone from their will or revoke their trust fund. There were no broken martini glasses on the Italian tile floor.

Finally, when Elise couldn't eat another bite, she used baby wipes Zane's sister offered to clean her hands and walked out onto the back lawn to stretch her legs. Zane had gone into the house for something. In the backyard, Elise watched the twin boys play on the tire swing. They were wearing paper pirate hats someone had made for them from newspaper. Her gaze shifted to Grandpop Keaton, seated beneath a big apple tree. Zane had pushed his wheelchair down the ramp, off the porch, and parked it beneath the sweet-smelling tree boughs because he said his grandfather loved the scent of apple leaves.

Glancing at the porch, but seeing no sign of Zane, Elise hesitantly approached the elderly Mr. Keaton. "Hi," she said, feeling a little funny talking to him. What if he didn't understand what she was saying? But Zane did say they didn't know. "My name's Elise. I—" She pointed in the direction of the house. "I'm Zane's friend."

To her surprise, the old man shifted his cloudy blue-eyed gaze to her. She wasn't certain, but he appeared to be listening.

She smiled and crouched beside his wheelchair taking note that someone took great care in dressing him. He wore a bright teal golf shirt, khaki shorts and a green ball cap that said John Deere across the brim.

"You have a nice place here." She looked up at the tree limbs above and imagined what it must have been to grow up here. From what she had heard at the table, Zane and his sister had lived here with their father and grandparents. She tried to imagine what it must have been like to have been Zane and Meagan and been surrounded with family who accepted them for who they were. Loved them.

She studied old Grandpop's craggy face, foolishly wishing for a moment he was *her* grandfather. "You have a very nice grandson," she said. "A nice family." She looked around the yard. "A nice place."

He seemed to be studying her face. Concentrating on her words. She sensed he wanted her to keep talking. What did she say?

"Umm…Zane took me out on his boat on the bay yesterday. Did he tell you? He showed the land that he said was your father's. Where you grew up." She hesitated. "Zane's asked me to look into the possibility that it might be for sale. You'd like that, wouldn't you? To have your father's land back in the family after all these years?"

He made no response.

She pressed her lips together, coming to her feet. "Well, I just wanted to say hi." She started to walk away, and she felt something touch her hand. It almost felt like a leaf at first. Dry. Cool.

Startled, she turned around and to see Grandpop Keaton's small, wrinkled hand in hers. Her gaze shifted to his worn, wrinkled face. He was smiling at her with bright white teeth. *At her.*

She smiled back, feeling a tenderness she didn't even know existed inside her.

Then he let go of her hand and turned his head ever so slightly away from her. Whatever connection they had made for that moment was gone.

Elise was still smiling when she entered house through the front door and went to the bathroom to wash the last hint of the smell of crabs from her hands. As she came out of the tastefully wallpapered old-fashioned bathroom, complete with a giant claw-foot tub, she stopped near Zane's office door at the foot of the staircase to study some family photos on the wall.

As she looked at the old school pictures of a young boy who had to be Zane, she heard his voice. He was in the kitchen talking to someone. His sister?

"Look, I'm not trying to poke my nose into your business," Elise heard the woman say.

It was definitely Meagan. Stay-at-home mom, Meagan, in her flowered long skirt, long, untrimmed hair and no makeup. Everything was about being a mother to her. All she had talked about at the picnic table was nursing the new baby, carpooling to school and soccer games. She was pleasant enough, but she seemed like a creature from another planet to Elise. They didn't live in the same world.

"But you shouldn't have invited her here," Meagan's voice cut into Elise's thoughts. "She doesn't fit in, Zane. Not in your life. Not in our family."

Elise held her breath, knowing very well who Meagan was talking about. *Her.*

Elise didn't know what to do now. Did she just walk into the kitchen and look Meagan straight in the eye? Did she go out the front door and around back to the porch and pretend she hadn't overheard Zane and his sister? Or did she make a run for it? Just get in her car and drive home. Better yet, go to the office and get some work done? When Zane called later to ask what had happened, she just wouldn't return his calls.

"You don't even know her," Elise heard Zane say.

"And neither do you. But you know women *like* her. Don't you?"

"I don't want to talk about Mom, if that's what this is about," he said angrily.

Elise heard water running in the kitchen sink. He had to be rinsing off dishes to put in the stainless steel dishwasher she had noticed when she'd been in the kitchen.

"How about Judy? You don't want to talk about her, either, do you?" Meagan asked pointedly. "Oh, for heaven's sake, Zane. She broke your heart! Why would you fall for this again? Didn't you learn your lesson the first time around? There are some women you marry and some you don't. And you're past the age of dating the don'ts if you're still serious about wanting a family some day."

Elise heard a pot clatter on the counter. More water.

"You're right. This isn't any of your business," Zane said, still angry. "This is my home and I can invite over anyone I want to invite. Besides, what are you getting your panties all in a twist about? She's just someone I met, that's all. I told you she was a real estate agent. She's going to see what she can find out about Great-Grandpop Keaton's land."

Just some real estate agent? That hurt as much as what Meagan had said.

"You can't lie to me. This is me you're talking to," his sister continued. "I saw the way you looked at her on the porch. Like you wanted to eat her up and wash her down with a beer."

Elise felt her heart give a little patter. His sister thought Zane was attracted to her?

Her mind skipped from disjointed thought to thought.

But who was this Judy? What did she have to do with his mother? What did either of them have to do with her?

Elise started to grow annoyed.

What right did Meagan have to judge her?

"Meagan—" Zane said.

"Look," his sister interrupted. "I've said my piece and now I'm going out on the porch to scoop ice cream. You do what you want."

"I will," he snapped. "And if I want your advice, next time I'll ask for it."

Elise heard the kitchen door open and shut and the

kitchen water continue to run. Zane was still in the kitchen.

Getting up her nerve, she walked into the hall from the office and into kitchen.

"Ellie?" Zane turned around from the sink and shut off the water.

She just stood there for a minute. She hadn't liked the tone of voice Meagan had used when speaking of her, and she hadn't liked what she had said. It had hurt. Zane was right, she didn't even know her. How could Meagan say Elise wasn't for Zane? And how could he have said she was just some real estate agent he was working with? Hadn't that kiss last night meant anything to him?

Apparently not.

He glanced at the screen door that led to the porch and then back at Elise. "You overheard that, didn't you?"

She nodded, her frustration blossoming into anger. In any of her previous relationships she would never have stood here. She would have walked out, ended the relationship before it ever had a chance to be one, and never said why. She could make an excellent ice queen when she wanted to. It was a Montgomery trait she had learned early on in life.

"I'm sorry," he said, walking around the butcher block counter to her.

She glanced at the door. "Who was Judy?"

He crossed his arms over his chest; his hands were still wet with dishwater. He leaned against the counter, studying her carefully. "My ex-fiancée. We would have gotten married last year. Fourth of July." He laughed, but it was obvious he saw nothing humorous in it. "She left two years ago for Singapore. A *job offer* she couldn't turn down."

At the tone of his voice, Elise lowered her gaze to her new white sneakers. A lump rose in her throat. She saw where this was going now. She wasn't the kind of woman Zane was looking for because she had a good-paying job? She was a career woman who had set goals for herself and achieved most of them?

Then, in the back of her head, she heard her father's voice. He told her she could never depend on someone else. Never really trust a man. Never make a relationship work; her career was what she had going for her. The only thing she had going for her. No one could ever love her.

She glanced up at Zane, swallowing the lump. "You ought to be ashamed of yourself," she spat. "Talking about me behind my back."

"Ellie—"

"Don't you *Ellie* me," she snapped. "Meagan doesn't know me well enough to judge me like that. She has no right. Not any more than I have the right to judge you because you're a chicken farmer!" She took a step closer to him, feeling her anger burn in her cheeks. "And as for your little comment about me being just some real estate agent you wanted to do some work for you—I just want you to know that I appreciate you warning me right up front that you were never interested in me, only what I could do for you!''

"Ellie—'' Zane shook his head, taking a step toward her, his hand out.

She sidestepped him. "Thank you for the afternoon. I had a lovely time.'' She strode away, headed for the back door. "You can keep the damned mushrooms!''

Still seething, Elise marched into her apartment, down the hall and into her office. Spotting *The Husband Finder* checklist with Zane's name scrawled across the top, she balled it up in both hands, ignoring the word "good heart'' written in her own handwriting.

"I knew this wouldn't work. It was a stupid idea,'' she muttered, throwing the ball of paper into the trash can. Then, like a true Montgomery, she sat down to work. She retrieved the messages from her voice mail and made a list of who needed return phone calls and what properties she wanted to schedule to show in the next week. She wrote her update for her Web page on Waterfront Realty's Internet site and e-mailed it to the Web master.

Still online, her fingers lingered over the keyboard. She thought about the boat trip the previous day and what a great time she had had. She tried *not* to think about Zane and how good he had made her feel or how wonderful his kiss had been. This was her own fault. The minute she found out he was a farmer and a family man, she should have dropped him. *The Husband Finder* was very clear in saying that men and women with similar work and home backgrounds made better partners. They simply had more in common, more to talk about. What did she have to say about chicken farming? What did Zane know about a woman working in a man's world, a man's business, and trying to get ahead? And what had made her think for a second that she could fit into a big family of in-laws?

Then Elise thought about Grandpop Keaton. About the beautiful land she had seen from the boat. She'd told him she would look into whether or not the property was going up for sale. It was a stupid thing to say; the old man probably hadn't heard or at least understood a word she'd spoken.

But she'd promised.

She typed in one of the best Web sites for information on properties soon to go on the market and reached for her computer mouse. She was doing this for Grandpop Keaton, she told herself firmly, not Zane.

"Sorry I'm not great company, tonight," Zane said, tucking his grandfather's dirty clothes into the hamper next to the bathroom door of his room in the nursing home. "It hasn't been such a great day." He walked over to the hospital bed where the elder Keaton sat on the edge, bony bare feet dangling.

Zane began to button up his grandfather's plaid pajama top. "Isn't it funny how you wake up some mornings thinking it's going to be one of the best days of your life—" He studied the cloudy blue eyes that seemed unseeing. "And then they turn out to be one of the crappiest?"

Zane buttoned the top button and smoothed the soft, worn fabric over his grandfather's thin shoulders. "I guess you know that girl I invited, Ellie, left in kind of a huff." He looked away, for some reason unable to meet the old man's gaze when he said it.

"Meagan and I were talking in the kitchen and Ellie overheard. She got pretty pissed off. You know Meagan and how overprotective she can be. She was afraid I was getting myself into another relationship like with Judy. It's not true, really. Ellie's not anything like Judy was." He paused. "Meagan's right, though. Ellie's whole life seems to be her job. She wouldn't have time for me. It's silly for me to get involved with her."

Zane met his grandfather's gaze. Was his grandfather looking at him? Really looking at him?

"The thing is, Pops, I really liked her." Zane couldn't tear his gaze from the cloudy blue eyes. "She made me feel…I don't know, different. I liked myself when I was with her. And she was funny. And she was incredibly smart. And for such a smart girl, there are so many things she's never done. Can you believe she's never been crabbing?"

Zane crouched down, pressing his hands to his knees to look up at his grandfather. "What, Pops? Is there something you want to say to me?'' He paused. Smiled when his grandfather didn't answer. It was probably just his imagination.

''Well, none of that matters anymore because Ellie gave me what for, and left. We won't hear from her again. And it's for the best, right?''

Then there it was again. Those eyes.

''You think I should call her?'' Zane groaned. ''I could apologize, but then what? She already thinks I'm a jerk. I start giving her this whole spiel about how afraid of career women I am because my mother abandoned us for a cigarette campaign, and my fiancée left me for a promotion and Elise will be giving me the name of a good psychiatrist.''

Zane sat down on the edge of the bed beside his grandfather again. ''No. It's for the best. I know you liked her, Pops, but Ellie and I, we just aren't meant to be. So I don't want to hear any more about her from you. Deal?''

Zane grabbed Grandfather Keaton's hand to shake it, but the old man wouldn't even squeeze it. He just kept staring and somehow Zane felt like a heel.

Chapter Five

For the contemporary woman, finding the perfect mate is not about emotion, it's about intellectual reason.
Don't be undermined by untrustworthy, messy sentiment.

Elise sat at her desk in her private office at Waterfront Realty, stared at the phone number written on her message pad, and chewed on the end of her Mont Blanc pen. Zane's number.

She needed to call him because he'd been absolutely right; the land where his grandfather had grown up was going up for sale sometime in the next two to three weeks. If Zane wanted to buy it, she knew his best chance would be to make a fair offer before it was officially for sale. Once it hit the market, a development company might come in and offer an outrageously high price to turn the bayside property into an exclusive housing development or condos.

The phone number seemed to leap off the page at her. It was his office number. There was no way she was going to call him at home. After all, if he had wanted to talk to her for personal reasons, he would have called sometime in the last week.

So why was she hesitant? This was strictly a business call, like one of the many she made every day. She and Zane had pretty much agreed last Saturday in his kitchen that they were not compatible. Just because he wasn't going to be her boyfriend, her "perfect mate," that didn't mean she couldn't be his agent and make a healthy commission off the sale of this property.

"This is ridiculous," Elise muttered to herself. "I'm not in junior high anymore." She punched the phone buttons with the end of her pen. "Come on, Ellie, you're a professional."

Ellie? Where did that come from?

"Farmer in the Dell Enterprises, how may I direct your call?" asked a pleasant receptionist on the other end of the line.

Elise had a crazy impulse to just hang up and gripped the phone tightly in her hand. "I am not in junior high," she lipped silently as if that was her mantra.

"May I help you?" came the voice again.

"Umm, yes, Zane Keaton, please. This is Elise Montgomery." It suddenly occurred to her that he might not take her call. "Returning his call," she finished quickly.

"One moment, please."

Elise sat in her leather chair behind her desk listening to a kiddy version of the song "Farmer in the Dell" coming through the line. "Cute," she muttered sardonically. "Really cute, Zane."

The phone clicked on the other end. "Hi, Ellie?" It was Zane's way-too-sexy voice, confused at the moment. "The receptionist said you were returning my call?"

"I apologize for misleading her," she said coolly in her best professional tone, "but I needed to speak with you, and I was afraid you might not take my call if you heard it was me."

"Don't be silly, I'm glad you called." He paused for a second. "Listen, I really wanted to call you this week and apologize again for Saturday. I—"

"Zane, this isn't a personal call."

"Well, I'm making it a personal call!"

His words took her by such surprise that she didn't have time to respond before he went on.

"The truth is, I wanted to call you and I should have. I've just been really busy."

He took a breath, and it was the perfect place for her to jump in. Just tell him she wasn't interested in what he had to say because she wasn't interested in him, and then jump right in with the information she had on the property, but he was too quick for her.

"No," he went on. "I haven't been *that* busy. I have your phone numbers in my pocket, and I've looked at them so many times in the last week that I've got them memorized. The truth is, I was just afraid you wouldn't want to talk to me. You were pretty angry when you left my place."

His voice sounded so sincere, so genuine. A man who could actually say he was afraid of rejection by a woman? Elise could feel her resolve weakening, but she fought it. Maybe because she was even more afraid of rejection than he was.

"*Zane,* I didn't call to talk about our disastrous date. I have a meeting in five minutes that I need to get to," she lied, "so do you want to hear about the property or not?"

"The property?"

"The property you showed me when we were out on the bay. You said you wanted to buy it when it came up for sale"

"Pops' land?" He sounded so surprised. "I can't believe you still looked into it."

"I'm a woman of my word," she said indignantly. "I told you I would and besides, I promised your grandfather."

"I know, but after that fiasco at my place, I just assumed—" He halted in midsentence. "You promised my grandfather?"

She took a deep breath, feeling silly. No, not silly,

just uncomfortable. For some unknown reason her chest had tightened with emotion. There was something about Zane's grandfather that had touched her. Touched a place in her heart that she didn't know very well. "We were just talking…well, you know what I mean and…I don't know, I told him I would look into it."

"Wow," he said, only the word came out tender.

Elise barreled ahead; there was way more messy sentiment involved in this phone call than she had intended, and she wasn't very good with emotion. Another Montgomery trait. "The land was owned by a Mr. Leonard Jacobs, but of course you knew that because he's probably the man you tried to talk to about buying it."

"The man with the chicken grudge," Zane interjected.

"Anyway, he died a few months ago, and his heirs are getting ready to put the property on the market." She doodled on the legal-size pad she kept notes on.

"You're kidding me! That's great. I mean, not great that he died, great that the heirs want to sell."

Elise looked down at her notepad to see that she had written Zane's name next to hers and drawn a heart around it. She couldn't believe she had done such a thing! She scribbled it out frantically. "I called to let you know that if you're interested in having me represent you, I can make arrangements for you to meet with the Jacobs' family estate lawyer." She hesitated. ''Of course if you'd rather work with someone else, I can suggest Liz—''

''Rather work with someone else, of course not! And yes, I'm interested, very interested. Wouldn't that be something if I could take Pops out to his old place? Push him around in his wheelchair under the same trees where he played as a boy?''

Zane sounded more like a kid than the CEO of what Elise had learned this week was a multimillion-dollar company. All she'd had to was Google him and the information had popped up. President and CEO of Farmer in the Dell Enterprises, an organic poultry and poultry products conglomerate that sold goods worldwide. Somehow the idea that he was such a successful businessman had knocked her for a loop. The only truly wealthy men she had ever known, besides her father, had been his colleagues and they had all been cookie-cutter cutouts of Edwin Montgomery. Every one of them was a workaholic with great business sense and no people skills. Cold fish right down the line, even with their own families.

Zane was nothing like her father.

''So when can we get started?'' Zane asked, knocking her out of her zombie world and back to the present.

''Umm.'' She was flustered now and that was so unlike her. Nothing ever flustered her; she was at her best under pressure. ''I'll have to make a couple of calls and get back to you.''

"Sounds great. You have my home and work numbers, but let me give you my cell number."

Elise wrote down the number beside the crossed out heart on her notepad. "I'll get back to you," she said anxious to get off the phone before she said something she shouldn't, like *I'm really sorry about the other day, too. I can understand where you're coming from because I apparently have some preconceived notions that might not be accurate. Want to get together for dinner and talk about it? Better yet, would you just like to come to my place and make out?* Instead she said, "Have a good day."

"You, too. And hey, Ellie?"

The way he said her name made her heart skip a beat. She wondered if maybe she was premenstrual. This whole physical reaction to Zane was so unlike her; she never even cried at Hallmark card commercials. "Yes?" Her voice sounded oddly breathy in her ear.

"Thanks so much. I can't tell you how much this means to me. What it will mean to Pops."

"You bet." Elise dropped the phone on the cradle as if it were too hot to handle and then stared at it for a second. For the first time in the past five minutes she felt as if she could catch her breath again; she exhaled slowly.

So that was that. Although Zane had apologized once more, he didn't say anything about seeing her again. Not that she would have agreed to go out with him. She was following *The Husband Finder*'s advice and wasn't wasting her time anymore with relationships that could go nowhere. It was just that...

"Get back to work," she told herself. "Work is where it's at when you're a Montgomery."

So Elise kicked her high heels off under her desk and threw herself into her day's to-do list. She didn't come up for air until two hours later when she heard a knock at her door. "Elise?"

She looked up from her desk to see Liz dressed in a sharp gray suit with her hair pulled back in a tight chignon. "Bring it in," Liz said to someone behind her.

Elise's eyes grew wide at the sight of a huge bouquet of bright flowers in a crystal vase, carried by a deliveryman.

"Oh, my gosh," Elise breathed, slipping her feet into her shoes under her desk and getting out of her chair.

"You've been holding out on me," Liz sang. "And you said you didn't think you'd go out with Bob the Broker last night. Start a fresh *Husband Finder* checklist did we? Must have been a nice evening." She drew out the last word as if Elise had found the man of her dreams.

"I didn't go out with Bob. He had appointments, I had appointments..." She let her voice fade away, unable to stop staring at the flowers as she pointed for the young man to set them on her credenza. Who could they be from?

Zane. They had to be from Zane. Only Zane would

send a girl a vase of wildflowers. The most beautiful flowers Elise thought she had ever seen. They looked as if they had been picked from a country roadside.

"Thank you," she breathed as the deliveryman left.

"So who are they from?" Liz snatched the card with the name of the florist imprinted on it from the plastic holder before Elise could get to it. "You're the best. Love, Zane and Tom?" She arched a plucked brow.

Elise fought a grin as she snatched the card from her friend's hand. "It's not what you think," she said tartly, sliding into her leather executive chair and slipping the card into the center drawer of her desk.

Liz planted her hands on her slender hips. "No, then what is it?"

"Business. Nothing more." Elise reached for her notepad and her pen.

"You sure?"

Elise didn't look up, but pretended to scan the paper in front of her, carefully covering the scratched out heart with her and Zane's name in it with her hand. She'd just die if Liz saw it. "I'm sure it's just business, now will you excuse me? I have some calls to make." She reached for her phone.

"You're making a big mistake," Liz sang as she sashayed out of the office. "It will never work. That book was right about one thing, you know, you have to go for men who are your type and that *chicken man* is definitely not your type."

Elise glanced up. Ordinarily, she would have just

held her tongue and let that comment go by, but she couldn't. "How do you know what type of man is right for me? I'm not even sure I know. What if what I *thought* I wanted isn't really what I need in a man at all?"

"Honey." Liz leaned on the door frame. "Do you hear yourself? A man's not supposed to change you. He's supposed to complement you—like a nice pair of designer shoes or a purse."

Elise glanced down at the notepad under her hand.

"You know what kind of woman you are and you certainly know what kind of man Zane Keaton is," Liz continued, an edge to her voice. "Look at him. Look at that sister of his. He doesn't want an equal. He wants a wife he can keep barefoot and pregnant down on the farm."

"That's unfair, Liz. You don't know him."

"I've known plenty of men like him. Remember Elliot?" She raised a brow. "The guy was great, money, nice car, nice house. By the third date he was talking marriage, the fourth, babies and by the fifth he wanted to know how far into my first pregnancy I'd be continuing to work. He had me an old married drudge before he got past second base with me."

"Zane is not Elliot," Elise said firmly, irritated by Liz's whole attitude. She was supposed to be her friend. Weren't friends supposed to be supportive? "Besides, this whole conversation is moot. I am not dating the guy. I'm setting up a sale that could possibly drop my name on Gallagher's desk. You know I've been itching to talk about that partnership.''

Liz frowned. "Look, I'm not trying to tell you what to do, Elise. I'm just trying to keep you from making the same mistake I've made before. That was the whole point of your checklist, to move beyond casual dating and find a man to get serious with.''

Realizing she wasn't going to be able to make Liz understand why she was questioning herself, realizing *she* didn't quite understand, Elise knew it was time to end the conversation. "Well, I certainly appreciate your concern for me." She forced a smile, though she was irritated with her friend and obviously Liz was irritated with her. This was the closest they had ever come to a fight.

"I better get back to work," she said, putting the phone to her ear. She didn't hang it up until Liz disappeared down the hallway.

An hour later her phone rang. "Elise Montgomery," she answered, cradling the phone on her shoulder while shuffling listing papers on her desk.

"Ellie."

"Zane." Before she could help herself, she smiled, dropping the paperwork and grabbing the phone. "Thanks for the flowers, but you really didn't have to do that. I sell property for a living. Making these kinds of deals is what I do.''

"You're welcome. I'm glad you liked them.''

A moment of silence hung between them, but oddly enough, it wasn't an uncomfortable silence.

"Hey, listen, I did want to be sure the flowers arrived," Zane said. "But I was also calling with a request—for my real estate agent."

That was better. Back on safe ground again. "Yes?"

"Have you talked to that lawyer yet?"

She leaned back in her chair. Usually she was a multitasker. She could talk on the phone, make entries on her PDA and scan the competition's ads in the newspaper while she talked. But she didn't want to do anything else; she wanted to give Zane her complete attention. "Not yet. I'm waiting for her to return my call. Why?"

"I was wondering if it would be possible for you get permission for us to go have a look at the property. You know, before I made an official offer. Ordinarily, I'd just go, but the last time I walked through there, old man Jacobs ran me off with a nineteen twenties sawed-off shotgun." He chuckled.

Elise didn't even react to the shotgun, she was still back on him wanting permission for *us* to inspect the property. Did *us* mean him and her or him and someone else? His sister maybe? "You and your lawyer?" she asked.

"No, me and my real estate agent. I want your professional opinion. I mean, I want the land for sentimental reasons, but I plan on using it to expand the research division of my company. I know part of the property has been declared a wetlands and I'd like to study my options."

Go with him, as in see him again outside this office or a lawyer's office? She didn't know what to say. When she'd done her research on the property, it hadn't occurred to her that she might have to see him alone again.

Her gaze drifted to the huge bouquet of flowers beside her desk, and she felt her cheeks grow warm.

It was silly for her to get herself all hot and flustered over Zane again. It made sense to keep this complete business—transactions on the phone, or across a desk. "I'm not sure I'm the person to help you on that front. Mostly I do residential."

"Aww, come on," he said lowering his voice, making it even sexier. "I'll take you for a ride in my truck. Bet you've never ridden in a seventy-nine 'F' one-ten pickup." He sounded so darned charming.

"I'll have to see what I can do." Her tone was all-business, but inside she could feel herself melting.

"Give me a ring as soon as you know."

"Okay—talk to you soon."

Elise was still smiling when she walked out of the office at 5:00 p.m. sharp, which, considering the fact that she didn't come in until 7:00 a.m., was barely a day's work by Montgomery standards.

She didn't know what had gotten into her.

Zane Keaton?

The following day after work, a Friday, Elise allowed Zane to pick her up at home at six, but she didn't invite him to come upstairs to her condo. That would have made it seem too much like a date. The plan was that they would go look at the property, and he would bring her directly home. She told him she had dinner plans, preempting any thoughts he might have had of dinner. And it was true, she did have plans, a bag of popcorn, a diet soda and Conan.

"Hi," Zane called out the open window of his pickup as he rolled up to the curb in front of her condo building.

She felt like he was watching her, sizing her up, as she came down the sidewalk and she didn't know if that was good or bad. Was he taking a second look?

She'd dressed and redressed three times. Ordinarily she wore a business suit and heels to show property, but that didn't make sense. She was going to be out tromping through woods and open fields, terrain not conducive to skirts and high heels. In the end, she'd chosen a pair of jeans—the only pair she owned, a white T-shirt and the sneakers she'd bought at the dollar store.

"Nice place." Zane glanced up at the pink stucco condo building inside the gated property.

She dropped her briefcase on the floor of the truck and slid in on the bench seat that was covered with a beach towel. She tried to situate herself on the lumpy seat before reaching for her seat belt. "Thanks." She tugged on the belt, but it wouldn't give an inch.

Without being asked, Zane reached across her and gave the belt a good tug, his fingertips brushing the tops of her thighs as he drew it back and fastened it beside her hip.

There was that doggone chemistry the book had warned her about again. Light-headedness. That spark of electricity that leaped between them. She tried to remind herself how fleeting sexual attraction was.

"The condo was an excellent investment. It's already increased in value by thirty-three percent." She held up both arms until his hand was safely on the steering wheel again, then lowered them to her lap.

"So you didn't buy it because you liked it?"

She sensed criticism in his voice and wondered if it was real or imagined. With her father, it was never imagined, but she wasn't really sure how to read Zane. He was so different than the other men she had known, dated, that all bets were off. This was definitely new territory she was entering.

"My father taught me that financial decisions should be based on reason, not emotions," she explained. "You're a successful businessman, surely you understand that?"

He shrugged his broad shoulders. He was wearing another surfing T-shirt with a wave whooshing across the front. This one, pale blue, matched his eyes perfectly. Shorts and a pair of old sneakers that looked as if he had owned them for twenty years, and a pair of fashionable silver wraparound sunglasses completed the ensemble. He didn't look much like a millionaire. He was entirely too hot.

"I always try to make sound business decisions,

but sometimes you just have to go with your feelings. Sometimes how you feel isn't about reason, is it?''

She stared out the window wondering if he was referring to how she felt about him, or the advice in the copy of *The Husband Finder* still sitting on the nightstand beside her bed. But that was silly, of course. He knew nothing about the book or how she felt. She gazed out the window, slipping on her sunglasses. ''That's not been my experience.''

Zane nodded thoughtfully as he turned out of the condo parking lot, through the iron gates, past the guard shack and onto the main road. ''You have family, Ellie?''

''Just a father in Texas. He owns an oil company. My mother left when I was young.'' She heard stiffness in her voice. She didn't know why she had mentioned her mother. She didn't usually talk about her with anyone.

''Mine, too. I guess you caught that in that conversation I had with Meagan. Mom and Dad divorced when we were young. Dad died of cancer last year. Meagan and I are still close with his family, though. My cousins at the house Saturday are all his brother's and sister's kids. Then, of course, I have Pops.'' He glanced in the rearview mirror and then at her. ''But I really miss my dad. It must be hard living so far away from yours.''

Elise had chosen to go to college in the east to get away from her father and his critical, manipulating ways. When he had refused to pay her tuition unless she pursued her academics in Texas, she'd gone to the University of Maryland and paid her own tuition by working nights and weekends.

"I'm not close to my dad," she said quietly.

"I see. I'm sorry to hear that. I thought—"

"Let's go over the details of this property before we get there, shall we?" She pulled a folder from the briefcase she'd brought along. "According to the last survey, there was ninety-seven and a half acres." She flipped through some photocopies she'd had made at the courthouse. "But the previous survey done in 1973 said there was ninety-three and a half acres, so I'll have to look into that. I also need to look into the zoning and that wetlands designation. You're going to have to be specific about how you want to use the land so that I can be sure you'll get county approval."

For the next twenty minutes, Elise successfully steered the conversation away from anything even remotely personal. She and Zane discussed the particulars of the property and its assets, as well as its shortfalls. She was pleasantly surprised by his knowledge of property acquisition and his overall business sense. Zane may have inherited The Farmer in the Dell from his father and grandfather, but it was obvious that it was *he* who had transformed the business from a mom-and-pop chicken coop operation, to a company that according to reliable sources, would soon go public.

She was impressed, but not for the reasons a Montgomery should have been impressed. Elise admired

OFFICIAL OPINION POLL

ANSWER 3 QUESTIONS AND WE'LL SEND YOU
2 FREE BOOKS AND A FREE GIFT!

0074823 |||||||||||| |||||||| ||||||| FREE GIFT CLAIM # 3953

YOUR OPINION COUNTS!

Please check TRUE or FALSE below to express your opinion about the following statements:

Q1 Do you believe in "true love"?

"TRUE LOVE HAPPENS ONLY ONCE IN A LIFETIME."
○ TRUE
○ FALSE

Q2 Do you think marriage has any value in today's world?

"YOU CAN BE TOTALLY COMMITTED TO SOMEONE WITHOUT BEING MARRIED."
○ TRUE
○ FALSE

Q3 What kind of books do you enjoy?

"A GREAT NOVEL MUST HAVE A HAPPY ENDING."
○ TRUE
○ FALSE

YES, I have scratched the area below.

Please send me the 2 **FREE BOOKS** and **FREE GIFT** for which I qualify. I understand I am under no obligation to purchase any books, as explained on the back of this card.

309 SDL DZ3Y   209 SDL DZ4F

FIRST NAME

LAST NAME

ADDRESS

APT.#

CITY

STATE/PROV.

ZIP/POSTAL CODE

(S-R-04/04)

www.eHarlequin.com

Offer limited to one per household and not valid to current Silhouette Romance® subscribers. All orders subject to approval. Credit or debit balances in a customer's account(s) may be offset by any other outstanding balance owed by or to the customer.

how much of himself Zane seemed to have retained in his climb to success. He seemed so ordinary in so many ways. When she'd started her *Husband Finder* checklist, "ordinary" was not a word she would have used as one of the qualities necessary in a man she could love, but Zane was making her think about some of those requirements. What she had said to Liz was true. She was beginning to wonder if she really knew what would make her happy.

"Well, here we are." Zane pulled off the main road, onto a rutted, weed-choked dirt driveway, put the truck in park and grinned. "Already feels like home."

For the next hour and a half, Elise traipsed through the weeds, climbed over fallen logs, ducked under low-lying branches and listened to Zane rattle on excitedly about his plans to expand his company. As the time flew by, she had to continually remind herself this was just another business meeting, but she kept coming back to how much she was enjoying herself. How much she enjoyed Zane, and she got the feeling that he felt the same way.

As they headed back to the truck, the sun beginning its descent over the bay, he walked closely beside her, his hands stuffed in his pockets. He had removed his sunglasses so she could get a better read on his mood by looking into his eyes. He seemed to want to say something, but was hesitant. Finally, just before they reached the truck, he spoke.

"Hey, I know you said you had plans tonight,

but..." He stopped at the passenger side door and rested his hand on the handle in front of her, preventing her from getting inside. "But are you absolutely sure you can't go out for a quick bite?"

She glanced up into his blue eyes and she could feel herself trembling inside. "To talk about the land?" she said.

"Umm, yeah, sure. Of course." He hesitated then shook his head. "No. Actually, Ellie, I think I'm asking you out on a bona fide date. I don't care about the land." He gave a wave of dismissal. "I mean I do, but I already knew I wanted to buy this land at any price—"

"Let's not tell the seller that," she teased, surprised by her playful reaction.

He grinned. "The truth is, I asked you if I could have a look at the land because I wanted an excuse to see you again. I haven't been able to get you out of my head, not since the night we met."

She bit down on her lower lip thinking about the things he and his sister had said in the kitchen at his house. Zane knew what kind of woman he wanted and it wasn't her. Wasn't this the mistake Liz had been warning her about earlier?

Zane laughed when she didn't respond right away. "Look, I'm making a mess of this, but what I'm trying to say is that I really like you, Ellie. I'm sorry about what happened with Meagan and I'd like a second chance."

That chemistry kicked in in an instant. Her palms went sweaty. She could almost *feel* his mouth on hers.

"And I'll be perfectly honest. Everything that is logical, that is reasonable in my head tells me you're not the woman for me. My good sense tells me that you're the kind of woman who is going to choose her work over me *every time,* but then…" He took her hand in his and pressed it to his chest. "Then this happens."

Elise could feel his heart pounding beneath her fingertips. She could feel the warmth of his skin, smell that intoxicating cologne of his again.

"So what do you say?" he murmured as he gently removed her sunglasses, his fingertips brushing against her temple and sending little shivers of pleasure through her whole body. Just that one touch.

Fighting the overwhelming feelings of attraction that washed over her, she looked up into his blue eyes, determined to be firm. That determination lasted until his mouth brushed hers and then it crumbled at her feet.

Elise felt her lips part of their own accord and she sighed with relief as she felt the pressure of his kiss. Somehow she ended up against the truck, her back pressed to the warm, smooth metal of the door. She slipped her free arm around his neck and groaned as his kiss deepened and the ground seemed to come up from under her.

She wanted the kiss to last forever, this moment in

the twilight, surrounded by the open fields and the warm breeze off the salt marsh.

"Just dinner?" he whispered as he drew his mouth from hers, still pressing her hand to his beating heart.

She closed her eyes and then opened them, thinking she was going to have to dig her checklist out of the garbage and find a place to pen in "most romantic moment," even if it was just in the margin.

"Just dinner," she agreed, tipping up her chin to gaze into his eyes again. She felt as if she was stepping off a precipice and free-falling. "And maybe one more kiss?"

Chapter Six

Family, friends and associates at work may know you better than you know yourself. If they don't approve of your new love interest, take a hard look at him. They may be right.

A month later, Elise found herself at home on a Saturday afternoon, instead of at the office. Early in the day, she'd gone to the gym, then the grocery store, then come home to clean up a little. In the past few weeks, she'd been so busy between work and seeing Zane that she felt as if she was falling behind, and her life was just a little bit out of control. It wasn't necessarily a bad thing, just very different from the life she had led pre-Zane. He was so spontaneous, and she was such a planner that everything he said and did seemed to delight her.

What did not delight her was the dry cleaning piled in her closet, the dust on her living room end tables and the fact that she couldn't remember the last time she'd mopped the kitchen floor. She had pending work at the office, too, and a contract proposal she needed to write that her boss was waiting for.

Instead, she was at her kitchen sink, barefoot with wet hair from her recent shower, repotting Gerber Daisies she'd bought on impulse at the grocery store.

The phone rang and she grabbed it off the counter, hoping it was Zane. They'd made plans to go out on his boat this afternoon, but hadn't set a time.

"Hi, there," she said smiling.

"Elise Anne?"

She hid the disappointment in her voice. "Father, how are you today?" She tamped down the black potting soil around the newly planted daisies with the spoon she'd used to stir her coffee this morning and then stood back to admire her work.

The pot was a homemade piece of pottery Zane had bought for her at an outdoor craft show. Thrown on a pottery wheel, it was blue and gray with streaks of green and didn't go with a thing she had in the house. She loved it.

"I tried you at the office," her father said, his disapproval plain in his voice. "I spoke with that pleasant young woman, Liz. She said you hadn't been in the office and weren't expected today."

"No…no actually I had some things I had to take care of." She picked up the potted plant and padded barefoot down the hall to her office where she had a southern exposure window. Zane had teasingly explained to her last week—after tossing her last attempt in the garbage—that plants needed water *and* sunlight.

"You weren't in the office last Saturday, either."

She set the pot in the windowsill and drew the miniblinds up to let plenty of sun in. "I'm sorry I missed your call. I left a message with your secretary. Zane and I went to Assateague Island to see the wild ponies. He couldn't believe I've lived on the east coast almost ten years and I'd never seen them. You know they are thought to have originated from a Spanish shipwreck off the coast."

"So you're still seeing him?" There it was again. The disapproval.

She gave the pot of daisies a final adjustment and plopped into the chair at her desk. "You'd really like him, Father. He's a businessman like you. I told you, he owns his own company. In ten years, he's brought it from a roadside stand to the international arena."

"Has Waterfront announced their June sales awards?"

She pressed her lips together. They'd been announced almost two weeks ago; she just hadn't wanted to get into it with him. "Yes, they did. Liz won. She's the one you spoke to on the phone. She made an incredible sale to—"

"Not working Saturdays. Gone before six in the evening. Elise Anne, I don't have to tell you what it takes to be successful."

She leaned back in her chair and stared at the tile ceiling. No matter how old she got or how far from Dallas she lived, he could reduce her to a chastised child in an instant. Only once, she would have just sat here and taken it. She stiffened, setting her jaw.

"I am successful," she insisted. "Just because I didn't win the sales award for the month doesn't mean I'm not good at what I do. Winning the sales award five months in a row was a fluke. It's never happened in the history of the company and will never happen again. Didn't I tell you that if the land deal for Zane works out, I think I have a good shot at being asked to buy into the company."

"Ah, I see." It was all in his tone of voice. Disapproval one moment, glowing endorsement the next. "So that's what this business is with this man." He chuckled. "You stand to gain a lot."

She picked up the *Husband Finder* checklist that she now displayed on her desk right next to several sales award trophies and a stack of plaques she'd never had time to hang on the wall at the office. She knew she should tuck it away in a drawer; she'd be embarrassed for Zane to see it, but she liked looking at it. She liked looking at his name.

She gently smoothed the wrinkles of the papers; battle wounds from the checklist's brief time in the garbage can under her desk. She smiled as she traced, with her finger, the words she had scribbled across the front page "good heart."

"Exactly," she said. "I stand to gain a lot."

"Well, I'm glad to hear you're using your head and not depending on any less reliable resources." He paused. "Monique is making the divorce more difficult than I had anticipated. She refuses to simply sign the documents. There have been tears. Fuss."

"I'm sorry to hear that. You and Monique seemed well suited for each other. Are you certain you can't work things out? Sometime marriage counselors can—"

"Montgomerys do not see counselors," he interrupted. "And we keep our dirty laundry to ourselves. Monique is making a spectacle of herself, and I guarantee that she'll regret it when she goes to cash her divorce settlement check."

"I just hate to see you alone again," Elise mused and she truly meant it. No one should have to live their life alone in a big empty house, not even a grumpy old man like her father.

"Must go," he declared briskly. "Fax me the details of the partnership, and I'll have one of my lawyers look it over. One can never be too careful."

"Thanks, Father, but I'm still not sure if—"

"Call coming in on another line. I'll call the office next Saturday. Have a successful week."

"You, too," she said, but he had already hung up.

Elise dropped the phone and stared at the folder bulging with information she needed to review before drawing up the documents Mr. Gallagher was waiting for. He expected them Monday morning.

She chewed on the inside of her lip. She had already told Zane she would go to church with him and his grandfather in the morning, and then they were planning on taking Pops to the beach. Zane wanted to try out one of those big wheelchairs the city offered that was built to roll over the sand. Then there was supper at Meagan's house. It was really important to him that she and his sister get to know each other, still insisting they would be great friends if both of them weren't being so stubborn.

Elise glanced at the phone. Suddenly, the work on her desk seemed to be looming. Frowning, she picked it up and dialed Zane's cell number.

"'Lo?"

"Hi, it's me."

"Hi, beautiful. Great minds think alike. I was just going to call you. You ready to go out on the boat and add to that nice tan you're working on?"

She was pleasantly embarrassed. She'd never had a tan in her life and she'd lived at the beach for five years. Since she and Zane had been dating, she'd bought a bottle of suntan lotion and had already used half of it. She'd never spent so much time in her life just…having fun.

"Actually, that's why I was calling." She gave the stack of paperwork a nudge with her finger. "I'm not going to make it today. I've got a ton of work here to do."

There was silence on the other end of the line.

She pressed her lips together and went on. "I know I said I could go out this afternoon, but I really need to get to work on this project. I've barely started it, and it's due Monday morning."

"Ellie, we talked about this," he said. She could hear the tension in his voice.

"I know."

"We both agreed that if we were going to give this a try, we were both going to have to respect the others' baggage."

She bristled at the word *baggage*. He might have emotional baggage but she certainly didn't! "It's been a busy week," she said firmly.

"I agreed not to say much about that fact that you seem to be doing everything others want you to do—"

He meant her father, of course. Maybe Liz sometimes. Definitely her boss. The self-help books?

"And you agreed to try and be respectful of the plans we make and keep them."

"I'm sorry, Zane," she said testily. "But I've already lost two deals this month because I was off windsurfing and keeping you company while you fixed your water pump. I have to make a living you know!" She didn't mean to shout those last words, but they came out that way just the same.

He was quiet again.

She felt like she was holding her breath.

"It's okay," he said then.

She exhaled. This was the first argument they'd had since they started dating again. She should have known it was bound to come sooner or later. In this business, she just couldn't work a regular nine-to-five, five-day-a-week job. "You sure?" She was hesitant. "I think if I really put my mind to it, I can finish it up by tonight. Then I'll have all day tomorrow to spend with you," she said hopefully.

"Hey, it's fine." It wasn't quite the pleasant, warm voice she was used to, but it was close. "You're right. I apologize for losing my cool. Things come up."

"Yeah, they do. So I'll see you at church in the morning?" she said hopefully.

"Pops and I will be there."

"Okay…" She felt as if she wanted to say something else. The words "I love you" were right on the tip of her tongue. But they'd never discussed love. She wasn't even sure that was what she was feeling here and she certainly couldn't speak for how Zane felt about her.

"See you then," she said softly.

"Bye, Ellie."

She hung up and stared at the file she'd brought from work with loathing. She didn't want to work, she wanted to play. She wanted to play with Zane.

But as that great philosopher Mick Jagger once said, "You can't always get what you want."

"Well," she said in her best Edwin Montgomery voice. "It's not going to jump up and get completed on its own is it, Elise Anne?'' She grabbed another file and hunkered down for a long afternoon of boring real estate work.

Zane walked through his sister's back door and into her kitchen where he found Meagan stirring a pot on the stove. The room smelled heavenly of tomato sauce and garlic. ''Hey, you have room for one more at the dinner table?''

She looked over her shoulder and smiled. ''For you little brother, always.''

He gave her a peck on the cheek and walked to the refrigerator to see what he could find to drink. It was a hot July day. He'd been in his garden picking sweet corn to take to his neighbors. He'd hoed his cucumbers and tomatoes while he was there, and then fertilized the limas. He was always one to throw himself into good hard physical work when he was pissed. And he was definitely pissed that Elise had canceled on him. Disappointed and pissed. Disappointed because he really wanted to see her, but pissed because he could see how easily this relationship could head down the wrong road, and it wouldn't be because he hadn't been warned.

''I'm glad to see you,'' Meagan said, ''but you do know you're a day early for Sunday's fried chicken and dumpling dinner, right?''

He grabbed a diet soda from the fridge and plopped down on a stool at her counter. She had a big eat-in country kitchen that she had decorated whimsically with old tin signs advertising eggs for sale, and ceramic chickens she'd been collecting since she was a little girl.

"We'll be here tomorrow, Ellie, Pops and I. I just stopped by to say, Hi. I wondered if maybe you and Ted might want to go out, either for dinner or a movie later. I thought I could watch the kids for you. I know you guys haven't had a minute alone since the baby was born."

Meagan turned away from the stove, the wooden spoon in her hand. He noticed that it was four o'clock in the afternoon, and she still hadn't had her shower. She was wearing a pair of baggy gym shorts that belonged to Ted and an old T-shirt that had seen better days. He loved his sister dearly, but he couldn't help noticing that since she'd thrown herself so far into the role of being the stay-at-home mom that she seemed to be losing her previous identity.

Meagan had once been the kind of woman who wouldn't have left her bedroom without her hair clean and brushed, and wearing makeup. Now, he couldn't remember when he'd last seen lipstick on her, even in church. Of course she did have the new baby, and four kids were a lot, especially when your husband worked odd hours.

"Go out?" She laughed. "Ted and I haven't been out since Justin was born three years ago. I don't know where we'd go out to!" She shook her head with amusement as she turned back to the spaghetti sauce. "Ted wouldn't go to a movie anyway. No remote."

"You could just go for a walk on the beach. Go out for an ice-cream cone. Talk. It's going to be a beautiful evening."

"Talk? Ted and I?" Again, she laughed. "Besides if you're talking about anything after 7:00 p.m., you know I'm nearly ready for lights-out. By the time I wrestle these little monsters into bed, I'm too beat for lively conversation."

He sipped his soda and shrugged. "I just wanted to offer. You know I always get a kick out of staying with the kids."

"Well, they love you, that's for sure. You're going to make a great daddy someday, bro." She smiled as she set down the spoon and went to the fridge to get a head of lettuce and an armful of fresh salad veggies she'd grown in her garden. "But it's Saturday, isn't it? I lose track of the days." She waved a carrot. "You don't have a hot date on a Saturday night?"

He set his soda down and came around the counter to help her wash the vegetables. "Ellie has something going on tonight."

"Work?" Meagan intoned.

He glanced at her and grabbed a tomato from her hand to run it under the faucet. "You promised you'd give her a chance, Meagan. I really like her." He hesitated, rubbing a spot on the tomato, then looked up at her. "I think I might be in love with her."

"Oh, Zane," she groaned, brushing a lock of straggly hair out of her eyes. "Please don't say that.

You've barely been dating a month. You can't possibly—''

''I'm telling you, I love her, Meg. I loved her the first time I saw her at that benefit dinner. I can't help it.'' He grabbed a knife from the drawer and began to slice the tomato and toss the cut pieces into the wooden salad bowl she'd set on the counter. ''She's so smart, and funny.'' He grinned. ''Better yet, she thinks I'm funny.''

''Stand-up comedy does not a marriage make.''

''She makes me smile,'' he said, sifting through his own feelings as he said the words aloud. ''Just hearing her voice. Seeing her walk out her door, knowing she's going to be all mine for the evening. I can't explain how good that makes me feel. And she's so persistent. She's hit roadblock after roadblock trying to buy that land for me and she doesn't give up.''

''Please tell me this is not some kind of misplaced sentiment based on Great-Grandpop's land.''

''No, it's not misplaced sentiment!'' He slapped the knife on the counter and turned to Meagan. ''Aren't you listening to what I'm saying? I'm in love with Ellie. She's the woman I think I want to spend the rest of my life with. And I want you to like her. Hell, I want you to love her, too, but I'm not going to let you decide who I will and will not love. Who I'm going to marry.''

Meagan reached for a dish towel and leaned back against the counter as she dried her hands. ''Zane, I'm not trying to give you a hard time here. You're right. I don't know Ellie very well, but I did know Judy well, and I liked her all right.''

"You did not. You thought she was selfish and single-minded.''

"I did not. But from the beginning, I knew she wasn't the woman for you because she was never going to give you what you needed. I'm afraid you've fallen for another woman just like her, that's all.''

He picked up the paring knife again and began to peel the cucumber. "Ellie is nothing like Judy.''

"Fine.'' Meagan raised her hands and walked away.

"Fine,'' he agreed with a nod. "Now go get dressed and go for a walk. Go to the grocery store. Do *something,* Meg. I'll stay here with the kids and get dinner on the table.''

She halted in the doorway. "I love you, little brother, you know that, don't you.''

He didn't turn around, but he smiled. "I know.''

It was after ten when Elise heard a tap on the door. Actually, it was more like a scratch. She'd just about completed the work on the contract for Mr. Gallagher and needed to reread it, but she'd decided she was starving and had gone to the kitchen to see what she could dig up. So far, she'd found a dill pickle, half an old sesame bagel and something that resembled Chinese food in a cardboard box in the back of the fridge that had turned a putrid shade of blue. Slim pickings.

Elise dumped the box of unknown identity into the sink, hit the disposal button, dropped the box in the garbage can and walked out into the hall to the front door. "Who is it?"

"A guy who makes a lousy boyfriend," Zane said from the other side of the door. "But I come bearing gifts."

She unlocked and opened the door, smiling. "Hey."

"Hey." He leaned over and kissed her mouth, lingering.

"Mmm," she sighed. "So you come bearing gifts? What kind?"

He held up a plastic grocery bag. "Homemade spaghetti and fresh garden salad with poppy seed dressing I made myself."

"Oh, bless you," she breathed, grabbing the bag from his hand. "How did you know I was starving? I was just trying to figure out how to make a sandwich out of a pickle and half a bagel."

He chuckled as he followed her into the kitchen. "I was going by on my way home from the nursing home and I just thought you might need a little fuel."

"How's Pops?" She pulled the containers out of the bag and popped the one with sauce into the microwave.

"Oh, he's good. I laid out his clothes for church tomorrow and he seemed to understand what I was doing. He always liked church." Zane leaned on the counter and chuckled. "Or at least the big chicken and dumpling dinner afterward."

She rested her hips against the white countertop across from Zane in the galley kitchen. "I'm glad you came by. Glad you brought food." *Talk about bonus round on the checklist.*

"So, you get done what you needed to?"

She nodded thinking how handsome he looked in his khaki shorts, faded polo and suntan. His sun-bleached hair fell over one eye giving him that bad-boy movie-star appearance. "Just about. Another hour, tops, and it will be ready for Gallagher's desk."

He crossed his arms over his chest, glanced at the microwave, then at Elise. "I wanted to apologize for today."

She shook her head and stepped closer. "You don't have to."

He reached out and rested his hands on her hips. "But I do. That was asinine of me to go off on you like that. It's the first time it's even happened. I guess I'm just overly sensitive."

"Because of Judy," she offered.

He nodded.

"Well, I'm probably oversensitive when it comes to work. I don't even know that it's work. It's just…" She glanced away, unable to meet his gaze.

"Tell me," he said softly, coming closer.

The microwave beeped, but she ignored it. She slowly lifted her gaze to meet his and fiddled with the collar of his shirt. "My father called today."

"And made you feel about an inch high."

She looked down.

"Ellie, I don't understand why you listen to him."

"Because he's my father."

"I know." Zane brushed her cheek with his fingertips. "I understand you want to be accepted. I'm just afraid that whatever you do, he's never going to be happy, Ellie. Not as long as you're not in Texas running his business with him. Letting him run your life."

Elise closed her eyes. Was what Zane was saying true? In the past few weeks, maybe even months, the same thought had passed through her mind, but she just didn't want to consider it. "Can we not talk about this right now?"

"Sure." He pulled her into his arms and kissed the top of her head. "Mmm. You smell good."

She pressed her cheek to his chest and listened for a moment to his beating heart. Then she lifted her head and met his mouth. She tightened her arms around his neck and pressed her body to his. He smelled so good, like sunshine and spaghetti sauce and a future she had been afraid to want up until a few weeks ago.

Zane's tongue teased hers and she groaned with pleasure. He stroked her back and then slid his hand down over her shorts to cup her buttocks. When they came up for air, he dropped his hand, looking a little sheepish.

"Sorry about that," he said, brushing the hair out of his eyes. "Got a little carried away."

She laughed realizing their relationship was heating up a notch. "You didn't hear me protesting, did you?" She gave him a quick kiss on the mouth. "See you in the morning?"

"You bet."

For a second he didn't let go and he acted as if he wanted to say something else. As she gazed up into his blue eyes, the "L" word was on the tip of her tongue again. She wondered if it was on his and her heart gave a little trip.

He released her and walked out of the kitchen. "I'll let myself out."

"Thanks for the spaghetti," she called after him as she reached into the microwave wondering where *"brings you homemade spaghetti when you're starving"* was going to fit on the checklist.

Chapter Seven

*Don't adapt your lifestyle to his. Focus on who
you are and your self-worth. Changes in your
lifestyle to suit a man should set off alarms.*

The first week of August, Mr. Gallagher called Elise
into his office.

"You wanted to see me, sir?"

A small man in his early sixties with graying hair
and an angular face, Joe Gallagher looked up from
his desk. "Sit down, Elise." He gazed at her over the
rims of his bifocals. "How's your week going?"

"Excellent, sir. I sold a condo at Mallard Lake and
the Brenner property at Lake Shore." She eased into
one of the leather chairs in front of his desk, feeling

a little nervous. One didn't get called into senior partner Joe Gallagher's office often.

"That the three bedroom with the purple kitchen?"

She smiled. "One and the same."

He nodded. "Listen, Elise, I've gone over July's
numbers, your July numbers, in particular." He
grabbed a sheet of paper from a stack on his desk.
"You were going so strongly the first five months of
the year that I'd be lying if I said I wasn't a little
disappointed."

She could almost feel her shoulders sag. "Business
has been a little slow."

He looked over the rims of his glasses at her again.
"Everything all right at home?"

"Fine. Yes, of course."

"It's just that you seem a little preoccupied. I
haven't seen you in on Saturdays and Sundays the
way I used to." He smiled kindly. "We don't close
this joint down together the way we used to."

She smiled back, but when she spoke, her tone was
testy. In Joe's chair, she saw her father and she didn't
like it. She didn't like the way she let him make her
feel. "I hadn't realized we had required weekend
hours, Joe, unless we were hosting an open house.
I'm here Monday through Friday, nine to five. I'm in
the office or out showing property."

"No, no, no, I wasn't suggesting you weren't putting in your required hours, only that you...well, hon-
estly, Elise, with Marshall's retirement and selling out
his share of Waterfront, the remaining partners have

been discussing offering one of our agents a piece of the pie, shall we say?"

She glanced up, not as pleased at mention of the partnership as she thought she would be. This was what she wanted, what she'd been working her butt off for five years for, wasn't it?

"I'd be very interested, Joe."

"I know you would, but so are Liz and Ralph. Now all three of you are in contention, and my favorite has been you all along. But I have to tell you, Liz took the July top sales award. That's two months in a row. You don't want her pulling too far ahead of you." He chuckled.

She didn't. "No, sir."

"So how is that property transaction for Farmer in the Dell going?"

She twisted her foot in her loafers. She'd bought a new suit with pants rather than a skirt and it had become her office "uniform." She couldn't get over how much more comfortable pants were than a skirt. She wondered why she had ever switched in the first place. Was she crazy? Sure, the male clients liked the long legs under the table but it was hard for her to believe that had been her prime reason for purchasing an entire closet of skirts and jackets.

"The city zoning commission is really dragging their feet, and we've still got this family feud going on between the seller's heirs and our client's deceased great-grandfather," Elise told Joe. "I'm not sure we're going to be able to swing this one."

He glanced at the sales figures in his hand. "If you want to be considered for the partnership, you need this sale, Elise, to even continue to be considered. Another big sale—" he winked "—and I think I can convince the other partners that you're the man for us."

Elise rose from her chair. "Is that all you wanted to see me about?"

"That's it. Now, you need any help on the Farmer in the Dell deal, you give me a ring. In the meantime, do a little research on this company." He scribbled on a stick-it notepad, tore off the sheet and handed it to her.

She read what he'd written and glanced up. "Lindsborg Associates? Don't they build golf courses?"

"Could be coming to town. If they do…"

"They'll need a nice chunk of property," she said looking down at the paper in her hand again. "Thanks, Joe."

"You bet."

On the way out of his office, Elise ran into Liz. Since they'd gotten into the heated discussion over Zane, their friendship was no longer what it had once been. Elise was hurt that Liz wasn't happier for her. She couldn't understand why her friend was so caught up in what they had read in *The Husband Finder*. After all, it had been Elise's pet project to begin with. Liz hadn't even wanted to give it a try.

"Hey, congratulations on the July sales award," Elise said, feeling awkward.

"Thanks." Liz hugged her leather portfolio to her chest. Her pale yellow suit skirt was very short, and her heels very high, showing off her long legs to perfection. "So how have you been? I've…I've been so busy I haven't had time to give you a ring, and you know how crazy it gets in here."

"Sure I do." Elise smiled at her. "Especially when you're reaching for that sales award. It takes a lot of extra hours."

Liz nodded. "That it does. Of course it's not like I have anything else to do with my time. Anyone else to spend my time with."

Elise frowned and then looked up and down the hall to be sure no one was approaching. She took a step closer to Liz. There was something about what Liz said that made her realize she might have misread her. Was Liz jealous of her relationship with Zane? Or could it be something else? Had the competition for partnership in the firm become personal?

"I'm sorry, Liz, but I have to ask," Elise said quietly. "Have I done something to upset you."

"Of course not. Don't be ridiculous." Liz gave her a professional smile, and put her hand on Joe's door. "I better get inside. He's waiting for me."

Elise gave a nod and stepped back. "Sure, okay, but if you want to talk."

"Liz? That you out there, my number one salesman?'' Joe called from inside his office. "Time is money.''

Liz ducked into the office and closed the door behind her. Elise walked back down the hall to her own office and sat in her chair. But instead of starting to return her morning's messages, she called Zane. He'd told her last night he'd be out of the office all day inspecting, so she knew he was at one of the farms that produced eggs for his company.

"Zane Keaton,'' he answered the phone.

"Hey, Mr. Farmer in the Dell.''

"Hey, real estate woman.''

She could hear him smile.

"What's up?'' he asked.

"I don't know.'' She twirled the phone line around her finger. "Does something have to be *up* for me to call you?'' She kicked off one shoe under the desk and wiggled her toes.

"In the middle of the day? Yeah, pretty much. You okay, Ellie?''

She appreciated his concern and the fact that he already knew her pretty well. "Sure, just having a lousy day, and I guess I wanted to hear your voice, but if you're busy—''

"Never too busy for you. Actually, I'm sitting in my truck at the Quickstop. I just grabbed some lunch. Now tell me why your day is so lousy.''

She sighed. "The sales numbers came out and Gallagher called me into his office to chew me out in the form of a little pep talk.''

"That mean you weren't the queen bee last month?"

She bristled. "This is a very competitive business, Zane. I've told you that."

"I'm sorry," he said. "I didn't mean that the way it sounded. You told me your sales were down, but I got the idea that that was okay with you."

"It was," she confessed, "until Joe printed the numbers in black and white and plastered Liz's name all over our Web site where mine used to be."

"I'm sorry, sweetie, but I'm not sorry that you've been spending your time with me and not them."

She smiled. "Thanks."

"Any time."

"I better go," she said. "Phone calls to make."

"I'll call you tonight."

"I'll have to work here late, but I'm leaving at nine whether I'm done or not so call after I get home."

"You bet. Talk to you later." Zane made a kissing sound on the phone and then hung up.

Elise closed her eyes, savoring the moment. No one had ever made kissy sounds on the phone to her. Definitely not *Husband Finder* approved communication.

"I think I'm in love," she said to the empty room.

Elise worked until twenty after nine, spending more than an hour reading up on Lindsborg Associates so that when she called them to ask if they were looking into putting a golf course in the area, she'd sound reasonably intelligent.

As she stepped out the front door of the realty building and locked it behind her, she heard a car engine start and headlights flashed against the brick building. Who the heck was that? She wondered if she could find her pepper spray in her purse as she turned around to see who was in the parking lot.

Zane? He was in his BMW sedan and not the truck. She walked up to the car as he pulled up next to the curb and put down the window on the passenger side.

"What are you doing here?" she asked leaning in the window. "Everything okay? Pops?"

"Fine. You hungry?"

"Starved," she admitted.

"Get in. We'll grab something to eat and I'll bring you back for your car."

She didn't even have to consider his offer. She climbed into the car and tossed her briefcase in the back seat. "You been out here long?" She leaned forward and met his lips.

"Not too long."

"You should have called the office number and let me know you were out here," she said. "I always pick up. I feel bad that you were sitting out here waiting for me."

"It's okay. You told me you were going to work late. I just came by on the off chance you wanted to go out to eat with me when you called it quits for the night."

She covered his hand with hers. "Always."

He grinned and pulled out of the parking lot. "Burgers or pizza. Name your poison."

"Pizza."

"You've got it."

One look into Zane's eyes and the way he smiled at her and the sales numbers, Liz and the partnership slipped from her mind.

A week later, running late, Elise pulled into the parking lot of Pops' nursing home and grabbed the wrapped gift off the back seat of her car. It was already getting dark, and she was so late. She had promised Zane she'd be here. Practically running up the sidewalk, she flung her purse over her shoulder and flew through the automatic doors into the lobby.

"Good evening, Elise," the nurse at the front desk said cheerfully.

"Hi, Sue, could you buzz me in?" Elise hurried to the locked doors that led into the Alzheimer wing. "Thanks!"

The doors opened and she rushed through. She went straight to the family room where Zane said they'd be having cake and ice cream. The Keaton clan would be celebrating at Meagan's this coming weekend but Zane wanted his grandfather to have a "party" with the other patients. The room was empty.

"Oh, no," Elise groaned. She'd been stuck in a meeting at Waterfront. A mandatory meeting. Joe and the other partners seemed to have no respect for other people's time. Didn't they have family who depended on them? Needed them? Didn't they want to go home at the end of the day?

Elise turned down the hallway, headed for Pops' room. Halfway down, she ran into Meagan carrying baby Alyssa on her hip. "He's in Pops' room," she said. "Getting him into bed. Any kind of exertion seems to tire him nowadays."

Elise stopped in front of Meagan and reached out to grab Alyssa's hand. The little girl was the first baby she had ever known and she was so darned sweet. She clasped her chubby hand around Elise's finger.

"I can't believe I missed the party," Elise said, wiggling Alyssa's hand.

The baby laughed.

Meagan met Elise's gaze with a disapproving one. "You need to get your crap together, Elise."

Elise eased her hand from Alyssa. "Pardon me?"

"He called the office looking for you. He kept saying you wouldn't be late, not to this. They told him you were in a conference and couldn't be disturbed."

Elise rolled her eyes. "This meeting, it went on forever. I—"

"If you're going to break his heart," Meagan said. "I wish you'd get on with it and get it over."

"What are you talking about?" Elise demanded, tired of trying to be polite. "I was in a meeting and I couldn't get out." She gestured.

Alyssa began to fuss and Meagan jiggled her on her hip. "I have to go. Feeding time." She walked away.

"Meagan," Elise called after her. When she didn't turn around, Elise gave a wave of disgust. "Forget it," she muttered.

The truth was, Meagan's opinion hadn't changed since that chat in Zane's kitchen. She'd made up her mind that she, Elise, was a workaholic who could never be what her brother needed. Of course, according to Zane, Meagan hadn't liked Judy either. So maybe she was taking this too personally, Elise thought. Maybe Meagan would never be happy and she needed to stop trying to make Meagan like her.

Elise walked into Pops' room. "Hi, I'm sorry I'm late."

Zane was dropping clothes into the basket, his back to her. Pops was already in bed.

"We couldn't wait," Zane said with no emotion in his voice. "The other residents wanted their cake."

"No, it's all right. I'm sorry I couldn't get to a phone to call you and then by the time I got in the car, I thought there was no need to call your cell. I'd be here in a minute." She walked over to the bed and offered Pops his present. "Hey, handsome."

He glanced up. She could have sworn he smiled.

"Look what I brought for you. A present." She wrapped his wrinkled hands around the brightly wrapped gift box that she'd actually wrapped herself. No gift wrap service here. Of course the dollar store didn't have gift wrapping, but they had plenty of tape and bright-colored ribbons—at bargain prices.

"You need help opening it?" Elise asked, making

herself busy while Zane fussed around the room. She could tell he was angry with her, but how angry, she wasn't sure.

"Here we go," she said. She pushed Pops' finger in through the opening in the paper and pulled back, getting a satisfying tearing sound.

Pops smiled.

"Look what's in here," Elise said. She opened the lid. "Let's see…your favorite toffee. A red handkerchief because I know you like red. And look, it's a little stuffed dog that looks just like Scootie." She pushed the stuffed animal into Pops' hand and he looked down at it with interest.

Zane stood by the door, arms crossed over his chest, a frown on his face.

"Look, I'm sorry I was late," she snapped, balling up the wrapping paper and tossing it in the trash. "But I had a long lousy day in a series of lousy days, and I don't need you to make me feel worse. Don't you think I wanted to be here?" She indicated his grandfather who was still looking at the stuffed dog.

"I haven't said a thing," Zane said coolly.

"You don't have to. Your sister did." She pointed to the hall.

"I really wanted you to be here." He stuffed his hands into his jeans pockets.

Elise tucked the candy and handkerchief into the drawer beside the bed. "And I wanted to be here, but I couldn't get up and walk out in the middle of the meeting. Zane, my job could be on the line here if I don't step up to the plate. Do you have any idea how hard I've worked to acquire that land for you? Do you have any idea how many hours I've spent on that project?'' Her voice trembled with the last words.

Zane balled his hands into fists at his side. "Damn it, Elise. I was counting on you."

She looked up at him. "I was late." She threw up her hands. "I don't understand how that's a crime." She grabbed her purse off the bed and leaned over to kiss Pops' dry cheek. "Happy Birthday," she murmured.

"Where you going?" Zane demanded.

"Home!" She brushed past him in the doorway.

"I thought we were going out to dinner after Pops went to bed."

"Then I guess you thought wrong, Zane," she threw over her shoulder. "I'm tired. I'm going to take my thoughtless self home, take a hot shower and go to bed."

He watched Elise stomp down the hall, turn and disappear, then glanced back at his grandfather.

Pops was still holding the stuffed dog she had brought him. It was a nice gift. He obviously liked it. But Pops wasn't looking at the toy, he was looking at Zane.

"What?" Zane said "She was the one who took off. I had a right to be angry. She said she would be here and she wasn't." He flung his hand as he walked toward the bed. "She obviously cares more about her career than she does us."

Pops just stared, but there was something disapproving in his eyes. Even in his face.

"Man, Pops. You don't understand." Zane looked at the clean tile floor. "I guess the thing is I love her and I'm scared to death to do this again. To get hurt again, especially the same way. I guess stupid is forever." He lifted his gaze.

Pops was looking at him, actually focusing.

"But you think she's worth it, don't you? Worth the risk?" Zane glanced over his shoulder at the door. "She's probably gone by now. Knowing her, she's gone back to the office."

Zane studied his grandfather's face a moment longer. "Okay, fine, I'll go out there and look for her, just to prove it to you. Will that make you happy? Fine." He got off the bed and headed for the door. "I'll be right back."

To Zane's surprise, he spotted Elise's blue Toyota in the fading light of the parking lot. She was just sitting there. It didn't even look like she'd started the engine yet. He glanced behind him at the doors that had closed. With a groan, he cut across the neatly manicured lawn and walked up to her car. She was gripping the steering wheel, staring straight ahead and didn't even see him.

He knocked on the glass. "Ellie?"

Startled, she turned her head.

"Put down the window," he said, motioning.

She looked at him, then turned the key and put down the automatic window.

"Ellie, what's wrong?"

"What's wrong?"

She looked as if she'd been crying.

"What's wrong? You mean other than that my father thinks I'm a failure because I didn't make top salesman. That either my best friend doesn't like me anymore because she thinks I'm in competition for a partnership, or she's jealous I found someone I care for and she hasn't. That I've worked so hard to get that land deal for you, and it looks like the whole thing is going to fall through. That Meagan hates my guts."

"She doesn't."

"Well, if she doesn't, she gives a good impression of it." Elise wiped her red eyes with her hand. "And then there's you..." She glanced up. "But other than all that, there's nothing wrong at all."

"Me?" he said quietly, leaning in through the window.

"I don't know what to do with you," she declared, throwing up her hands. "You're not at all what I wanted in a man, but..."

"Well, thank you," he teased. One look at her teary face and his anger had melted away. He just wanted to hold her now. "But?"

She looked up at him. "I want this to work so badly," she whispered.

He opened the car door, took her hand and pulled her out. Holding her in his arms, he closed the door with his knee. "I want this work, too," he said, looking into her beautiful green eyes. "I want to make it work because I'm in love with you, Elise."

"You are?" she sniffed.

He smiled and placed his hand on her cheek. "This would be the time to say something else, like maybe you love me, too?"

She laughed, choked and threw her arms around him. "Oh, Zane. I do love you. I've known it for weeks, I just…"

"You just what?" He brushed her blond hair off her forehead. She had started growing it out since they began dating and he liked it this way. Softer. More feminine.

"I'm just so afraid I'm going to screw it up. That I can't make it work, that I can't make any relationship with a man work."

"Ellie, don't say that." He kissed her forehead. Her cheek. The tip of her nose. "Now listen to me. I don't want you to worry about that land deal. If it comes through, it comes through."

"But you wanted it so much," she said, looking up at him, searching his eyes. She was so beautiful, so vulnerable right now that all he wanted to do was protect her. Hold her.

"I did. But it won't be the end of the world if I don't get it. Pops is going to love me just the same whether I buy that land before he dies or not." He chuckled. "Shoot, I don't know that he'd know the difference. As for Meagan, she's just going to have to get over herself. She can't tell me who to love."

"I just want her to like me because I know how important family is to you." Her lower lip trembled. "And I don't have any family of my own. I've never had a sister."

"I know." He kissed her trembling lip. "And lastly, as for you screwing up this relationship, it takes two, doesn't it? So what's say we take it one day at a time, huh?"

She nodded.

He squeezed her tightly in his arms and closed his eyes, reveling in the feel of her, the smell of her skin and hair. "I love you, Ellie," he murmured, liking the sound of the words on the end of his tongue.

"I love you," she murmured.

Zane covered her mouth with his, kissing her soundly, and when he lifted his head, he heard the sound of clapping.

They looked toward the sidewalk of the nursing home and saw, in the twilight, three elderly ladies lined up on the bench clapping enthusiastically.

"It looks like we have an audience," Elise whispered, touching her fingertips to her lips.

He threw back his head and laughed, thinking how good it felt to love again.

Chapter Eight

*There's a honeymoon time early on in every re-
lationship. Don't get sucked into it. The honeymoon always ends and cold reality sets in
again. Keep your eye on the goal in choosing a
mate. Life is cold reality, not a honeymoon.*

Two weeks later, Elise hung up the phone and
squealed with delight. Then, embarrassed by her un-
professional outburst, she glanced up to see if anyone
in the hallway had heard her. She covered her mouth
with both her hands, grinning like a Cheshire cat.
"You did it!" she told herself, bouncing up and
down.

She grabbed the phone again and punched in

Zane's cell number, knowing her name now came up on his phone when she called in.

"Hey, Sugar Pie."

"Where are you?" she asked, when he answered. She was so excited she could barely breathe.

"I just left the office, headed home to pick the last of the sweet corn. Weatherman is forecasting rain, though it sure is beautiful out right now."

"Can you come get me?"

"Now?"

She knew he was frowning, those pale eyebrows of his knitted in confusion.

"At three-thirty in the afternoon on a Tuesday?" he said. "You okay?"

"I'm great! Better than great. I'll wait for you outside the office."

Ten minutes later, Zane pulled up in front of Waterfront Realty in his car. Elise jumped in the front seat, tossing her purse on the floor. "We got it!"

"We got it?" Then Zane's face lit up. "We got it!"

Grinning, she nodded.

"Ellie, that's wonderful!" He threw his arms around her in a bear hug. "We got it! I can't believe it! We got the land!"

She tightened her arms around his neck. "The tentative okay came in on the rezoning this morning, and the Jacobs' estate lawyer just called to say your last offer was accepted by the family, and his clients will be signing the sales contract tomorrow. You'll be settling on the land in a matter of weeks."

Zane kissed her on the cheek, then on the mouth before letting her go. "I can't believe you made this happen. Pops will be so happy—at least the family will be happy for him. You're good. You're very good."

She settled back on the car seat and grabbed her seat belt, pleased that he appreciated her professional capabilities. And Liz said he'd never get it. He got it!

"So, I was thinking," she said. "How about if we pick up Pops, grab something to eat and go have a picnic out on your about-to-be-acquired property? Right under that big oak tree where you said the old farmhouse used to stand?"

An hour later, Zane and Elise sat on a checkered blanket beneath that old oak tree. He had carried his grandfather from the car and Tom Keaton now sat under the tree where he once played on a tire swing and stared up at the tree branches with a joy on his face she hadn't known was possible.

"So what do you think?" Elise asked pushing a blueberry into Zane's mouth. They sat across from each other, cross-legged on the blanket spread beneath the tree. They'd stopped at his place, grabbed the blanket, raided the refrigerator and picked up the dog. Now there was almost nothing left of their fried chicken, marinated cucumbers and potato salad feast, but a plastic butter dish full of blueberries Elise had picked from Zane's hybrid patch in the backyard.

He kissed her fingertips and chewed on the berry. "I think this land is perfect for what I want it for, and Pops obviously thinks it's perfect." He motioned with his chin in the direction of his grandfather.

Pops sat in the grass, knees up, his back against the tree trunk with a cup of iced tea in his hand. He was grinning so hard she feared his dentures might come loose.

"I think he knows," she said, running her hand down Zane's broad back. "He knows where he is. Look at that smile."

"He does, I'm sure of it." Zane took her hand and lifted it to his lips, kissing each knuckle. "And I don't know how to thank you."

"You don't have to." She glanced at Pops then back at Zane. "That smile is enough." Elise leaned forward and kissed him on the lips.

"Mmm," he said, pulling her into his lap. "You taste like blueberries."

"So do you."

He kissed her again, running his hand over her bare suntanned legs. She'd actually worn a short jean skirt and a lime-colored T-shirt to work today, prompting Liz to ask her if she hadn't gotten a chance to go by the dry cleaners.

Elise was still upset that her friendship with Liz seemed to have disintegrated, but she hoped that with a little time, once Liz saw how happy she was with Zane, her friend would come around. Even so, Elise suspected that as long as they worked together the competition in the office would always create a strain in their relationship.

"Whoops, just a second." Zane got up and went over to the tree where his grandfather sat. The old man had fallen asleep, still holding his iced tea. Zane took the cup gently from his hand and set it safely aside.

"I wish you'd known him before," Zane said. "Before his memory began to go, Pops loved baseball. He took me to my first Major League game when I was seven. Pops was a hard worker, but some days, he'd take a notion and come looking for me. 'Zane, boy,' he'd say. 'All work and no play makes life no fun at all. Let's run off and do something that makes us laugh.' And we would, Ellie. We'd go fishing, or clamming, or even roller-skating. Once, he picked me and Meagan up early from school, and we spent the afternoon looking at mummies in a museum in Philadelphia. Pops might have been a chicken farmer, but he opened windows to the world for me and all of his other grandkids."

"You must have had a wonderful childhood," Elise said. She'd toured Europe one summer with a group from her private summer camp. She'd enjoyed the experience, but her father hadn't considered the trip "fun" for fun's sake, and his only participation had been paying the bill.

A crack of thunder sounded overhead and Zane glanced up into the sky. "Dark clouds. Weatherman was right—I think we better hit the road." He slid her off his lap, got up and offered his hand, pulling her to her feet.

They kissed again and she swayed in his arms, wanting to prolong the moment. She liked it out here on Pops' old farm. She'd never considered herself a nature girl before, but over the last weeks, between coming here and exploring Zane's farm, she discovered that she loved the smell of fresh-cut grass. She found that she liked picking blueberries and tomatoes, liked the feel of the freshly turned dark soil under her bare feet. She even enjoyed hunting for eggs in the henhouse. It was a like treasure hunt!

Another crack of thunder sounded overhead and Elise thought she felt a drop of rain. "You better get Pops," she said. "I'll clean up the picnic."

Zane released her regretfully and clapped his hands together. "Scootie! Let's go, boy! Train is pulling out!"

Elise laughed as the dog came bounding through the weeds, dragging a branch behind him that was bigger than he was. She packed up the remains of their dinner in an old picnic basket Zane found in the pantry. She folded up the blanket and tucked them both in the trunk with Pops' wheelchair.

The rain began to fall in earnest as Zane slid his grandfather into the back seat of the car and came running back to the tree to help her with the cooler of drinks and the dog dish they'd left behind.

"Oh, no," Elise laughed, lifting her palms heavenward. The sky seemed to open up and dump buckets of cool water on them.

"Run," Zane shouted above the thunderclaps, taking the cooler from her. Bright streaks of lightning zigzagged the dark sky.

Elise clutched the empty water bowl to her chest and made a run for the car. By the time she and Zane were safely inside with Pops and the dog, they were both soaking wet.

"Look at us," Zane said, wiping his wet face. "We look like drowned rats."

She glanced down and realized she was so wet that it made her T-shirt see-through. "Oh, no," she groaned.

He lifted a brow. "I don't know, I kind of like it. My own personal wet T-shirt contest."

She laughed and gave him a push as she tried to conceal the outline of her bra and breasts from him.

"What are we going to do with her, huh, guys?" Zane started the engine and laid his arm on the seat to look over his shoulder and back down the drive. "What are we going to do with Ellie?" he asked the dog and his grandfather. "Marry her before she wises up and runs away?"

A shiver ran through Elise's body and she hugged herself tightly, her eyes wide. Had Zane just said what she thought he'd said? She was so afraid to look at him that she just stared straight ahead through the wet windshield.

Zane turned the car around and pulled forward, down the dirt lane toward the road. He glanced at her.

Elise still stared straight ahead, watching the wipers, not sure what to do. What to say. What if she'd misunderstood him? What if he was just joking? But surely he knew she'd heard him.

They were several minutes down the road before she finally got the nerve to steal a peek. He looked over at her, that silly, handsome grin on his face. "This is the first time I think I've ever heard you this quiet," he teased. "I didn't mean to put a damper on the party."

She shivered and reached out to turn on the heat.

Zane looked at her again. "I love you," he said, sliding his hand across the leather seat as he focused on the road again. "I didn't mean to spring that on you that way. It just came out. We'll talk later, without the audience." He eyed the rearview mirror and his grandfather who was still smiling.

"I love you, too," Elise whispered, still waiting for her heartbeat to slow to a reasonable pace.

He squeezed her hand and she turned her head to look out the window at the passing fields, the rain running along the pavement. To her amusement, all she could think of was, *Well, Edwin, it sure paid to leave work early today....*

Elise and Zane took Pops back the nursing home and she waited in the front lobby while he gave his grandfather a warm bath and tucked him in bed in his favorite pj's with an episode of *Gunsmoke* playing on his TV. Elise kissed the old man good-night and to her surprise, he reached up and caressed her cheek. It was just like that first day at Zane's house when he had grabbed her arm.

"I love you, too, Pops," she whispered, tears filling her eyes.

Zane gave his grandfather a kiss on the cheek, and then arm in arm he and Elise walked out to the car together. The rain had stopped and the night air was cool and humid. She could hear the sound of crickets in the wet grass.

"I'll take you back to your car or we could just go back to my place," he said, slipping his arm casually around her waist.

She eyed him, feeling a little more comfortable now that her shirt had nearly dried. "Let's go to your place."

They were quiet on the ride to his house, but it was an easy, contemplative silence. Elise had never known anyone else that she could just be with without conversation or entertainment and be so content. At his place, they released the dog from the back seat and then walked up on the porch to sit side by side on the old-fashioned wooden porch swing that hung from the rafters.

Zane slid his arm around her shoulder, and they stared out into the darkness. The Lab ran in circles through the grass barking and then took off into the darkness.

"You know, I meant what I said today," he said smoothing her hair at the back of her neck, sending pleasant shivers down her spine.

"What you said?" She looked to him. Of course she knew exactly what he was talking about. She'd thought of nothing else since he said it, but she wanted to hear it again.

"About wanting to marry you." He rested his hand on her far shoulder and looked down at her.

She met his gaze and she could feel herself trembling inside. She had never gotten to the chapter on "The Proposal" or "The Wedding" in the book because she hadn't seen the point. Now she wondered if she should have read ahead.

"Are you asking me?" she whispered, holding her breath.

He thought for a moment and then grinned. "Yes, Ellie, I'm asking you. I'm totally unprepared." He laughed lifting his hand from her shoulder to gesture. "No ring, no speech. But it just hit me tonight in the car that I want us to be together. Always. I want to be your husband and all that means." He waited a moment. "So what do you say?"

She exhaled, dizzy from lack of oxygen. "Yes."

"Yes?"

"Yes, I want to be with you. Yes, I'll marry you." Her chest was tight, and she could feel her heart pounding, her pulse racing. "But only if you really mean it," she heard herself say. "I think you know me. You know who I am and what I am. Can you love me anyway?'' Her voice caught in her throat.

"Ah, Ellie. I do love you for who you are."

She lifted her mouth to meet his and felt her pulse quicken again. She parted her lips, inviting his tongue and drew closer. He threaded his fingers through her hair and kissed her until she was breathless, then kissed her again. His warm arms around her, he pulled her onto his lap and she ran her hand over his chest, reveling in the feel of his warm skin and his heart beating. As he lifted his hand to push the hair from her face to kiss her again, his finger brushed her breast and she sucked in a great gulp of air. The lightning that had been in the sky earlier now seemed to arc between them.

Zane had felt it, too. He took her mouth hungrily and she threaded her fingers through his hair. He drew his lips down over her chin, lower to the pulse of her throat.

"Ah, Ellie," He groaned.

"Zane," she panted. She'd always been so careful with men in the past. She kissed, of course, enjoyed the physical pleasure of it. But she never gave of herself, not of her heart. Not like this.

"Ah, sweetie." Zane exhaled, pressing his cheek to her chest.

They were on dangerous ground now. They both knew it.

"I want to make love to you," he murmured as he lifted his head to look into her eyes.

"I want that, too," she breathed.

He swallowed. "But I think we should wait. I think it's worth waiting for, don't you?"

She nodded, unsure if his words disappointed her or made her love him all the more. Both. She did want to make love with Zane, but a long time ago she had decided that perhaps her father sleeping with so many women was part of why marriage meant so little to him. And if she married, it would be forever. She wanted to be married to Zane forever.

"You're right," she whispered, smoothing his hair where she had tousled it with her fingers. "But we don't have to wait long, do we?"

He laughed. "How's this sound? My cousin Carter is getting married in South Carolina in a month. I was going to invite you anyway. How about if we announce our engagement then? All my family will be there. It will be the perfect time, and it will give me time to get you a ring."

Still sitting on his lap, she smoothed his cheek. She could feel the slightest bit of beard stubble on his chin, and she liked the sensation. "Sounds perfect."

"Now, it's a Saturday," he warned. "So we have to go down on Friday."

"It's not a problem."

"You're sure you can miss a couple of days at work? I don't want to tell everyone you're coming and then show up like bachelor number three."

She laughed. "I wouldn't miss Carter and Amy's wedding for the world."

"Then it's settled. What kind of ring would you like?"

"Whatever you pick out will be perfect. I think you know me better than I know myself," she confessed. "Just make it a surprise!"

"Surprise it is. Now come on, let me take you home." He slid her off his lap onto the swing, setting it in motion.

"I don't have to go yet." She looked at her watch. "It's still early."

"You do have to go." He got up off the swing and adjusted his shorts. "Because if you don't go, I'm going to pick you up in my arms and carry you up to my bed and ravish you. Now come on." He offered his hand.

Laughing, touched, she accepted his hand and followed him across the porch and down the steps. At this moment, she'd follow Zane anywhere.

The phone was ringing when Elise walked in the door. After taking her to her car and then following her to be sure she got home safely, Zane hadn't even walked her to the door. He said she was still too tempting, that he needed to stay away from beds tonight as long as she was near. They had kissed through his open car window. It was an innocent enough kiss but there was an exhilarating hint of anticipation in it.

"How do you feel about autumn weddings?" he

had called after her as she went up the sidewalk to her door.

"I love them," she called to him not caring if anyone heard her. "And I love you! Just make it early autumn."

He was still laughing when she slipped in her door and closed it behind her.

Elise picked up her phone, kicking her sandals that were still damp and now beginning to rub at her heel. "Hello."

"Oh, thank heaven!" Liz exclaimed. "Where have you been? I was afraid you'd been kidnapped or something."

"What?" Elise dropped both sandals on the living room carpet and left them there. She flipped on a lamp.

"I've been trying to reach you for hours. You car was still in the parking lot. We thought maybe you'd gone out to show some property and ridden in the client's car, but then you didn't even answer your cell."

As she padded down the hall toward her office, Elise thought about how she had tossed her purse in the back seat of Zane's car when he picked her up at the office. She'd never thought about it again until they returned to the office a short time ago to get her car. "I'm sorry, I didn't mean to worry you." She was actually touched that Liz had noticed she was gone and had worried about her. Maybe things weren't as bad as she thought between them.

"Gallagher was pretty bent out of shape when he couldn't get a hold of you. I think he left a hundred messages on your home and cell phones."

Feeling guilty, Elise glanced at her answering machine blinking in the dark on her desk. She flipped on the light switch, illuminating the room. "What did he need?"

"Some guy called from Lindsborg Associates." Liz sounded like she was reading the name off something.

"Lindsborg?" Elise had been so busy fighting for Zane's land, between that and her usual showings, she hadn't thought twice about Lindsborg Associates and their golf course since she talked to some guy in their acquisitions department almost two weeks ago. He'd said he would get back to her. She couldn't even remember his name—Stroudsburg, Stromsburg. She assumed she'd never hear from them again.

"That's what it says. Lindsborg Associates. A Robert Stroudsburg called twice for you."

"I'll call him first thing in the morning," Elise said, reaching for her *Husband Finder* checklist on her desk. She knew she had to come clean with Zane on it eventually, but she thought he might like to see it. She'd written all over it in different colors of ink and crossed out much of what the author had printed.

"Thanks for calling me, Liz. I'm sorry I made you worry."

"So exactly where the heck were you? Mark said

he saw you at the copy machine at three and then no one saw you again the rest of the day.''

"I made the Jacobs' sale. Zane is buying the land.''

"Wow, that's great. Congratulations. I told Joe you knew what you were doing there. I knew you were handling Zane Keaton just fine.''

"I wasn't handling him, Liz.'' She took breath. If she didn't tell someone, she was just going to burst. "He asked me tonight to marry him,'' she blurted out.

There was pause on the other end of the line. Brief, but definitely a pause. "What did you say?''

Elise was disappointed that her friend didn't sound happier for her. "I said yes, of course. This is what I've been waiting for my whole adult life. This is what we talked about, Liz.'' She looked down at checklist in her hand. "The book worked. The list worked.''

"Zane isn't anything like what you set out looking for.''

Elise tossed the paper on her desk. "I thought you would be happy for me.''

"I am. I am if you're happy,'' Liz backpedaled. "I just hope you know what you're doing.''

"So do I,'' Elise confessed thoughtfully, dropping into her chair. "So do I.''

Chapter Nine

*Serious lifestyle differences can spell disaster in
a marriage. Opposites may attract, but they
don't stick. If you're looking for a forever marriage, choose a mate with your own background
and ambitions.*

Joe Gallagher walked into the conference room of
Waterfront Realty and offered his hand to Zane who
was just rising from his chair. "You must be Mr.
Keaton," he said, taking Zane's hand and pumping it
enthusiastically. "Joe Gallagher, one of the partners
of this fine firm."

Zane looked to Elise who was sorting through the
papers on the mahogany table, taking care to be sure

each party received the properly signed forms. Zane wouldn't even have to go to settlement tomorrow as his lawyer was handling it for him.

"Nice to meet you," Zane said. "Elise has spoken of you."

"Well, we're very proud of Elise." Gallagher drew himself up to his full five-foot-nine frame. "She did a hell of a job on this deal."

Zane smirked, looking back at her again. "That she did."

"A smart woman," Gallagher went on. "Nice woman."

"I like to think so." Zane winked at her.

Elise eyed him. She hadn't told anyone in the office yet, but Liz, that she was engaged. She hadn't told her father yet, either. After all it wasn't official yet. It wouldn't be until next weekend when they announced it at the rehearsal dinner party, Friday night. Zane was giving her the ring, then.

It wouldn't be real until then, although they'd already picked a November first wedding date. Nothing fancy. They would be wed at the little country church that Zane had attended his entire life. Elise liked it there; she liked the people. And then, they planned a reception at the local country club that she hadn't even known Zane belonged to. He'd told her that he kept his membership just in case he needed a wedding reception. A cancellation had allowed them to make the arrangements on such short notice.

Elise shook her head ever so slightly at Zane, hoping he'd get the message. She knew he wanted to say something about their plans to marry to her boss, but she wasn't ready. Gallagher was still on the fence about her becoming a partner and he might not take the news well. Truthfully, she was on the fence, too. It was what she had wanted since the day she became an agent here, but now, she just didn't know. Owning a share of the company would be costly in money and time. She didn't want to work seven days a week anymore, ten, twelve hours a day. She wanted time to be with Zane. It was crazy, but after getting to know little Alyssa, she even thought she wanted a baby.

"You know, Elise and I are engaged," Zane said.

As the words came out of Zane's mouth, Elise wanted to leap across the conference table in her best pair of heels and cover that sexy mouth of his with her hand. She wanted to stuff the cat back in the bag. Instead, she just stood there, smiling pleasantly and stuffing the paperwork into the appropriate folder.

"Is that right?" Gallagher asked stiffly, seeming to puff up. "Well, congratulations." He looked to Elise and nodded. "I'm certain you'll be very happy together."

"Thank you." Zane grinned. "I know we will because I love Ellie very much."

Gallagher raised his bushy eyebrows. "Well, good to meet you. Elise, when you get a moment, could I see you in my office?"

"Sure."

Zane waited until Gallagher was gone and shut the door, leaving him and Elise alone in the boardroom. "You haven't told anyone?"

She closed her eyes and groaned. "You said we'd make the announcement at Carter's wedding. I just assumed—"

"How about your father?" Zane made no pretense of hiding his irritation. "You call Edwin?"

"We haven't been able to catch up with each other."

Zane made a sound in his throat.

"Zane, I've been really busy with this Lindsborg thing, and your paperwork, and those new spec houses off Route Thirteen."

He slipped off his gray suit jacket that looked so good on him that he could have stood in any boardroom in the world, even her father's. "Ellie, do you still want to marry me?"

"Of course!" She came around the table. "Zane, of course I want to marry you. I love you."

He looked down at her, his jacket draped over his arm, his mouth taut. "And I love you and I don't want to hide that fact. I want to tell everyone. I've *told* everyone." He threw out his hand. "I love Elise Anne Montgomery," he shouted.

She closed her eyes, pressing her fingertips to one throbbing temple. "Zane, I work here."

"So what? Real estate agents don't fall in love? Don't marry?" He was raising his voice again.

"Of course they do." She grabbed his hand, turning him to face her. "But men look at women in their jobs differently, and you know it. I have to be careful of my professional image here."

"Ah, so we're talking about your career?"

She looked up at him, searching his blue eyes. "I don't understand why you're angry with me. You said we would announce our engagement next Friday. That's less than two weeks from now. I was going to tell everyone when I got back, including my father."

Softening, he reached out to rest his hand on her hip. "I don't want you ducking out on me."

She shook her head. "I won't," she said softly, realizing that she wasn't the only one anxious about their wedding plans. It hadn't occurred to her that Zane might be worried, too. It was a big step. What person in their right mind wouldn't be? "No one is offering me a job in Singapore," she told him. "And even if they were, I wouldn't take it."

He grinned. "I love you."

"I love you, too." She lifted on her toes and kissed him. "Now get out of here because I have to go talk to Gallagher, and then I have a lot of work to do before I cut out of here at five."

He blew her a kiss from the door. "See you for dinner at Pops'?" It had become their weekly ritual. Every Monday, they had dinner—meat loaf—in the lounge with his grandfather and then took him for a walk on the grounds.

"See you at Pops' and I won't be late," she said. Elise watched Zane go, then gathered up her folders and walked down the hall. She knocked on Gallagher's door.

"Come in."

"You wanted to see me, Joe?"

"Close the door."

She pushed it with the heel of her shoe. As she looked at her boss and his bushy eyebrows, the thought occurred to her that she could quit this job. She didn't have to listen to what she knew he was going to say. She could just hand him the completed paperwork for the sale and walk out.

What would she do then? Anything she wanted. When she was in high school, she had wanted to be a teacher. Her father had insisted business was the only profession a Montgomery could succeed at. She was beginning to realize that he had been wrong about many things. He was probably wrong about that, too.

"So you're getting married?"

She nodded.

"Nice catch."

She eyed Joe. The comment wasn't worthy of a response.

He teepeed his hands, fingertips to fingertips. "I just want to be sure that you and I are on the same page, is all, Elise."

"I can do my job and be married."

He studied her over the rims of his bifocals. "Of course you can," he placated.

"Every man in this office is married, including

you," she said, "and I resent the insinuation that marriage might prevent me from doing my job."

"It's just that as a partner, Elise…" He opened his arms. "It takes a great deal of dedication." He pulled off his glasses. "Frankly, dear, if you'll excuse my crudeness, it takes balls."

Her irritation had turned to anger. How dare he suggest she didn't have what it took to make it in this business? She was a better salesman than anyone in this building. Hands down. She gritted her teeth. "I've got them, Joe. You know I have."

"It's just that I have to go back to the partners—"

"I think I'm going to swing this Lindsborg deal," she blurted out. She hadn't intended to say anything until she was sure, but he just made her so angry with his platitudes and bushy eyebrows that she hadn't been able to stop herself.

"Are you now?" The brows went up with renewed interest.

"The vice president of the company may fly in as early as next week to see the Johnston property. It's perfect for a golf course at the beach. The land's a steal, even at that exorbitant price," she told him proudly. And she was proud. It would be a good deal for both parties, and she and Waterfront would make a killing. Not that she really cared about the money, but her face would be back on the sales page of the Web site and even her father, who knew the Lindsborg courses, would be impressed.

Joe leaned over his desk, pressing his hands to his

blotter. ''You make this sale, Elise, and I think that partnership is as good as yours.''

''Fine,'' she said. She didn't even say thank you. She just walked out the door.

Two days later, the telephone on Elise's nightstand rang. She was already in bed, just drifting off to sleep. She glanced at the clock as she reached for the phone beside her bed. It was eleven-forty.

''Hello?''

''Ellie?''

It was Zane, but it didn't sound like him. There was something wrong. She sat up in bed and reached for the light. ''Zane, what's wrong, hon?''

''Pops.''

She heard his voice catch in his throat.

''Pops died, Ellie.''

''Oh, Zane, I'm so sorry.'' Tears welled in her eyes, not just for Zane's loss, but her own. She really had loved the old man, which was pretty amazing considering the fact that they had never once shared a verbal conversation.

''I left him about eight, tucked into bed with that stuffed dog you gave him.'' Zane's words were halting. ''The nurses called me a few minutes ago. They went in to turn off his TV. You know how he fiddles with the timer. And, he…he was dead. Died in his sleep.''

Elise scrambled out of bed and grabbed a pair of

gym shorts she'd left on the floor. "Where are you? Are you at home?"

"I'm going over to the nursing home for just a minute, meeting Meagan there."

"I can come."

"No, Ellie, it's okay. Go back to sleep. I just...I just wanted to tell you...because I knew you loved him, too." He took a deep breath, and she knew he was fighting not to cry. "I have to go. I'll talk to you in the morning. I love you, babe."

"I love you, too."

But Elise didn't go back to bed. She dressed and she got in her car and she drove to the nursing home where she spotted Zane's truck parked next to Meagan's station wagon. She grabbed her purse and hurried in the front door.

"Elise, hi." The night nurse smiled sadly. "Sorry about Tom. He was such a sweetheart."

She smiled and wiped at her eyes. "Thanks."

"Zane and Megan are still inside with him. I'll buzz you in."

Elise entered the dim room where Pops had slept for the last three years of his life. Meagan was just headed out the door, her hair a mess, her face red from crying.

"I'm so sorry about your grandfather," Elise said, reaching out to squeeze Meagan's hand.

She smiled. "Thanks." She looked over her shoulder to her brother. "I'll see you in the morning."

Zane, seated beside the bed where his grandfather

still lay, raised his hand. "We'll talk about arrangements, then."

Elise walked over and rested her hand on Zane's back. He sat in the chair, leaning over, his elbows on his knees, his face in his hands.

"You didn't need to come," he said, his voice muffled.

"I know." She looked down on Pops. She had always thought it was silly when she read accounts of how peaceful a person looked when they were dead, but she saw it now, and she smiled, sad and happy at the same time. Sad he had died, happy she had known him. Maybe a person had to love the deceased one to see that peace.

She continued to rub Zane's back. "But I wanted to come."

He lifted his head, wiped his eyes and stood. "I think I'm ready to go now. I've said goodbye."

She looked down at Pops' sweet face. "You don't want to wait until—"

He took her hand, shaking his head. "No, it's okay. He donated his body to science." He chuckled, leading her out of the quiet, dim room. "He made all the arrangements years ago. We'll just have a simple memorial service Sunday, after church probably. Maybe a fried chicken dinner." He laughed. "Something quiet. Pops wouldn't approve if his passing interfered with Carter and Amy's wedding. He always loved weddings. Loved dancing and kissing the brides."

Elise smiled at Zane's memory. Hand in hand, they

walked out of the Alzheimer's ward and out of the nursing home. In the parking lot, he walked her to her car. "You know, I wasn't ready…"

"Ready to say goodbye?"

"No," he shook his head. "But it was selfish of me. Pops was ready to go. It's just hard, parting with him."

She ran her hand down his arm. "I'll follow you home."

He didn't argue.

Back at his farmhouse, they walked hand in hand up the porch steps to find Scootie waiting for them. Zane patted the dog's head and pushed open the screen door for them.

"You want me to make you some tea or something?" Elise asked.

He halted in the kitchen and put his arms around her. "I'm pretty tired. I think I'll just go to bed."

"Oh," she said. "I can go home, I'll see you tomorrow."

He rested his cheek on her shoulder. "Ellie?"

She closed her arms around him. "Umm-hmm?"

"I know we agreed we'd wait until we were married to make love, but would you sleep with me? Just for tonight?" He lifted head, giving her that boyish grin she loved. "Just test out the old bedsprings?"

She smoothed his cheek with her hand. "I'd like that."

So still hand in hand, they walked up the stairs and lay down on the top of the homemade quilt spread across Zane's four-poster bed. With her cheek resting on Zane's shoulder, his arm around her, Elise drifted off to the most peaceful sleep she thought she'd ever know.

A week later, Elise was in her office trying to clear her desk. Tomorrow she and Zane were leaving for South Carolina, along with the entire Keaton family to witness Cousin Carter and his fiancée Amy's wedding. Elise was excited about going, but she was also nervous.

Pops' death the previous week had been hard, but in grieving for the loss of the new friend she had made, she discovered that she and Zane had grown closer. Somehow, sharing their personal pain made them more a couple. And his family had been so kind to her, even Meagan. Sunday, after the memorial service, they had gone back to the family farm to have chicken and dumplings the way Pops liked Sunday dinner, and Meagan had asked Elise to look after baby Alyssa while she fried chicken.

Elise had spent the whole afternoon with the baby, even spending some quiet time with Meagan sequestered upstairs while she nursed the infant. Elise came away from the day knowing she and Meagan weren't best friends yet, but they were no longer enemies.

Elise grabbed a stack of pending contracts and slipped them into the proper file in her filing cabinet. When she went back to her desk, she spotted a pink "While you were out" slip of paper dated from the previous Friday. She picked it up, walking around her desk as she read it. She knew she hadn't seen it before. It had to have gotten lost on her desk.

From: J. Lindsborg

Message: Great talking with you. Flying in next Friday. Make dinner reservations and we'll talk turkey.

"Oh, no," Elise groaned. "No, no, no." She crumpled the paper in her hand, afraid she was going to cry.

"Something wrong?" Liz stuck her head through Elise's doorway.

"Martha must have left this message on my desk last week. Somehow it got shuffled to the bottom of the pile."

"And the message is?" Liz asked.

"The vice president of Lindsborg Associates is flying in Friday to have dinner with me. John Lindsborg."

"So? Take him out, wine and dine him and go see Zane afterward."

"Liz, this is the weekend." She came around her desk. "We're going to Zane's cousin's wedding. We're announcing our engagement. Zane is giving me a ring Friday night."

Liz frowned. "You could call Lindsborg and reschedule."

"Reschedule when he's coming tomorrow?"

"No, I guess that won't work." Liz lifted her gaze. "So tell Zane you'll meet him down there."

"He won't understand." Elise shook her head, walking back around her desk.

Liz hesitated. "I know you don't want to hear this, but if he won't understand, he's not the man for you. This deal is going to make you a partner in this company. Does he have any idea what that will mean for your future?"

The piece of paper still clenched in her hand, she grabbed her purse from a desk drawer. "I'll be back in an hour," she said and she walked out.

All the way to Zane's house, Elise practiced what she would say. She'd explain the situation, tell Zane to go ahead without her to South Carolina, and she'd take the first flight the next morning. Zane would understand because he loved her. He would have to.

She pulled up in his yard under the trees that were beginning to drop their leaves. Only late September, it was still warm, but the air had changed and when she breathed deeply she could feel the changing of the season. She glanced up at the farmhouse as she walked toward the porch. It was so pretty, so idyllic. The other night they had discussed living arrangements after they got married, and she realized this was where she wanted to live. The family farm was where she wanted to raise their children.

"Zane?" She walked up on the porch where his dog welcomed her and she stuck her head in the kitchen. "Zane?"

No answer. He wasn't in the house, but his truck

and his car were in the driveway, so he had to be around here somewhere.

She walked back down the steps and around the house with Scootie following behind her, wagging his tail excitedly. She was dressed casually in crisp khaki slacks and a white blouse that seemed more suited to her mood these days than the slick, tailored suits that hung in her closest in their dry-cleaning bags.

"Zane?"

"Ellie? In the garden."

She walked around the back of the house to find him pulling up string bean plants, shaking the roots free of dirt and tossing them in a pile. He was wearing blue jeans, a green T-shirt and work boots with his wraparound sunglasses and he looked so good she could have eaten him up.

"Hi." She came down the row of beans.

"This is a pleasant surprise." He grabbed her by her belt loop and pulled her over, giving her kiss. "What's up?"

She looked at his dusty boots and then up at him. She wished he wasn't wearing the sunglasses so she could see his eyes. "I need to talk to you about tomorrow."

He took one look at her and his mouth hardened. "You're not coming," he said flatly.

"Zane—"

He pushed her aside and walked down the row of beans toward the house.

"Don't walk away from me! You haven't even

heard what I have to say," she called after him, her anger flaring.

"I've heard enough," he shouted back, "to know the engagement is off, Ellie."

Chapter Ten

As the relationship progresses, be careful of potholes in the road. Do not allow yourself to believe they're merely speed bumps. Heed those red flags and end a relationship before you become emotionally entangled.

Elise stood in the garden and watched Zane retreat in disbelief. "You're not even going to let me explain?" she demanded, following him.

"No explanation is needed." He kept walking. "You've made yourself perfectly clear."

She ran to catch up. "Zane, there was a mix-up with my messages. Lindsborg Associates' vice president called me almost a week ago to say he'd be in town Friday night. They want to go through with the deal. I can't *not* meet him." She grabbed his hand and he halted but he didn't look at her.

"Sure you can cancel."

Elise had never seen him this angry.

"Call the guy and tell him there's been a mix-up and that you won't be in town Friday night because you'll be in South Carolina with your fiancé attending a family wedding."

"Zane, I can be there by Saturday morning." She planted herself in front of him, blocking his path to the house. "I won't miss Carter and Amy's wedding."

"Their wedding isn't the point, damn it!" he exploded. "The point is *our* wedding. *Our* engagement. What you're doing is canceling our engagement."

"I'm not," she groaned in frustration, tucking back a lock of blond hair behind her ear. "I want to marry you. I want to tell your family we're officially engaged. I just can't be with you Friday night because I have this obligation."

"You can't be with your fiancé when he announces to his family that he's marrying you because you have a business appointment," he said coldly. "What? I'm supposed to announce our engagement alone?" He gave a humorless laugh. "Sounds to me like you canceling our engagement. Sounds to me like that golf course deal is more important to you than the ring I was going to give you!" He gestured angrily.

Elise looked down, and when she lifted her head,

her voice was full of an anger that matched his. She had known this was going to happen. She had known it! How could she ever have been so foolish as to have thought she could make it work? Her father warned her, Liz had warned her and even that stupid book warned her!

"Liz said you would respond this way," she muttered.

"Of course." He threw up his hands. "I knew *that* was coming. How about your father? Surely he warned you? Surely Edwin Montgomery told you you couldn't marry me and be happy. And of course you listened to them, didn't you?"

She crossed her arms over her chest, setting her jaw. "That's unfair and it's untrue."

"You can lie to yourself, Ellie, but you can't lie to me. You've spent your whole life trying to please others. Trying to be who others wanted you to be, do what others wanted you to do. Now you have to love who you're told to love?"

"You don't know what you're talking about," she ground out.

"I think I do. You've spent your whole life trying to get your father to accept you, to love you. And guess what, it's not going to happen. No matter what you do, he's not going to give you that love, because the old man doesn't have it in him." He opened his arms. "He just doesn't."

Elise felt tears sting the backs of her eyes, but she

refused to let Zane see her cry. "You don't know my father."

"Oh, I do. I know him because he's just like my mother! Ellie—"

This time it was Elise who walked away. "This conversation is over," she said. "If you can't accept the fact that I have obligations to my career, then we don't belong together."

She walked down the path, around the house. Scootie ran after her, the Lab darting in front of her, wagging his tail, licking her fingers. Ellie thought for sure Zane would follow her, too. He didn't.

She patted the dog's head and climbed into her car. "So that's that," she said. She wiped at her eyes with the back of her hand, started the engine and backed out. She had a lot of work to do if she was going to be ready for John Lindsborg by tomorrow night.

Elise remained at work that day until after ten at night and fell into an exhausted sleep. She tried hard not to think about Zane. She was heartbroken, but she knew it was better to break up now than later. She was determined she would not divorce and marry again and again as her father had. She'd remain single before she'd subject herself to that kind of emotional upheaval.

She and Zane just weren't suited to each other. It was that simple. Everything *The Husband Finder* had said was right; she'd just ignored all the advice, thinking she knew better. As for what he said about her listening to others instead of herself...well, he was just plain wrong. He was angry when he had said that; people said things that weren't true when they were upset.

The next day at the office, Elise wore her best knock-'em-dead red silk skirt and jacket, and her highest black heels. She was the first one in the office that morning.

When Liz arrived at nine, she walked into Elise's office. "So how'd it go yesterday with Zane?"

Elise had been filing some paperwork and she kept her back to her friend. "About as badly as it could have."

"I'm so sorry."

And it sounded as if Liz really was. Elise turned around to face her friend. The backs of her eyes felt raw, she'd been holding back her tears so long. She swallowed and smiled. She wasn't going to cry. "Thanks."

"So?" Liz lingered in the doorway.

Elise knew what Liz was asking. "So, the wedding is off." She walked back to her desk. "And I'm going to make this sale to Lindsborg if it kills me." She slid into her chair, and began to flip through some information she had printed off the Internet about some of the company's other golf courses.

"And you're okay?" Liz asked quietly.

Elise lifted one shoulder thinking that if she could just get through today, she'd be all right. "Nothing that good hard work and a great sale won't fix."

Liz laughed with her. Then she was quiet for a minute. "Listen, Elise," she said. "I want to apologize for my behavior the last few weeks."

Elise frowned. "I don't know what you're talking about."

"Yes, you do." Liz walked up to Elise's desk, forcing Elise to look at her. "The fact of the matter is, I was jealous. I was jealous that you had someone who cared about you and...and I was jealous that you're better at selling real estate than I am."

"Liz—"

"Let me finish, babe, because you don't get an apology out of Liz Jefferson often." She pressed her French manicured nails to Elise's desk. "I just want to tell you that I'm sorry. You're my friend and I should have been happy for you. You know, I laughed at you about that book, but secretly I was jealous that it worked for you."

Elise gave a snort. "Yeah, right."

Liz smiled. "You know what I mean. At least you're trying. You know what you want, and you're going for it." She tapped the desk. "Well, I'll let you get to work. Now, I want you to call me as soon as you leave Lindsborg and tell me all about the deal."

Elise smiled, pleased things were mended between them. "You bet."

That evening, Elise reached the restaurant early to be sure the table at the expensive seafood restaurant was just right. She ordered a mineral water and took a seat to wait for John Lindsborg. As she sipped her water, against her will, her thoughts drifted to Zane.

She couldn't believe he hadn't called her. He had said he loved her, and yet he had broken off the engagement so suddenly, so easily, that she wondered, had he really loved her at all? Had she never been the kind of woman he could love?

But then she thought of all the summer days they had spent on his boat, walking with Pops, just swinging on the front porch at his place and how much she had enjoyed being with him. He was funny, smart, kind; when she was with him, she had thought she was a better person than when she was apart from him. Wasn't that love, or had she misinterpreted love for "messy emotions" as *The Husband Finder* had suggested?

She sipped her water and watched the maitre d' escort a couple in their midsixties to a table across the dining room. They had to be husband and wife—they even looked a little alike. They were laughing as the husband pulled out his wife's chair for her. She smiled up at him, and the look on her face...it was pure love.

Elise wondered how long the couple had been married. Thirty years? Forty? How had *they* known they were meant for each other? How had they known they were in love and that their love would last? They had certainly not had any books like *The Husband Finder* to guide them. And from the look on their faces, she doubted their fathers or friends had told them they were in love and that their love would last.

Elise's eyes filled suddenly with tears.

She'd made a mistake. It was probably too late to fix it but—"

"Miss Montgomery," a distinguished man in his early forties said.

Elise rose from her chair, shaking his hand. "Mr. Lindsborg, it's nice to meet you."

"I can't tell you how pleased I am that you contacted us, Miss Montgomery. My father is very impressed with your—"

"Excuse me, Mr. Lindsborg—"

"Please, call me John."

"John." She grabbed her purse. "Could you excuse me for a minute? I'll be right back."

Before he could answer, she hurried off for the ladies' room. Inside, she glanced at herself in the mirror as she dialed her cell phone. She was an attractive woman; she liked her hair longer like this, not so stylized. But the red suit. It just wasn't her. Never had been.

The phone rang and Liz picked up. "'Lo."

"Liz?"

"Elise, what time is it? You can't possibly be done with your meeting with Lindsborg already."

"Liz, listen to me. How fast can you get over here to the restaurant?"

"What?"

"You heard me." Elise looked at herself again in

the mirror and smiled. "How fast can you get dressed in one of your power suits and be here?"

"I...I'm still dressed. I can be there in ten minutes."

"Perfect. You'll be meeting with John Lindsborg. He has a wife and three children. It's all in the portfolio along with the details of the land agreement, which I'll leave on the table for you."

"Leave on the table? What are you talking about, Elise? Are you all right?"

"I'm fine." She couldn't stop smiling at herself. This might not work. It probably wouldn't, but no matter what, the decision was her own. "I'm great, Liz."

"But where are you going? You've worked so hard on this project—the sale is practically in the bag. Why can't you meet with Lindsborg yourself?"

"I'm going to South Carolina to make an apology, and then I'm quitting my job."

"Quitting?" Liz asked, in obvious shock.

"Yup, I'm quitting." She leaned on the sink, not caring if she watermarked her silk skirt. "I don't like the realty business. Don't know that I ever have."

"But you're so good at it," Liz said. "You're the best."

"So I'll be the best at something else. Something I like."

"So you're going after him," Liz said quietly.

"I've probably ruined it. It's probably too late, but I at least owe Zane an apology."

"And he doesn't owe you one?" she asked. "He's the one who broke up with you over this whole thing to begin with."

"Well, love isn't about keeping score. And our breakup was a little more complicated than that. Listen, I'm heading for the airport."

"You're just going to leave? You're not going to pack? Get directions?"

"Nah."

"Boy, you've got balls, Elise Montgomery, I'll give you that."

Elise laughed, pushing though the ladies' room door. "I'll talk to you when I get back. Thanks, Liz."

"Thank you."

Elise hung up her cell and walked back into the dining room. "John," she said, approaching her table. "Something's come up, and I have to go."

He started to get out of his seat. "Is there something I can—"

"Please, sit. Have a glass of wine on us. I have to go, but Liz Jefferson, our top salesman last month will be here shortly. Now, all of the information you need is here in my files that I'm going to leave for her, so don't worry, you'll be in great hands." She picked up her leather briefcase from the floor and set it on the empty chair across from him. "It was very nice to meet you." She shook his hand. "And good luck with the golf course."

Elise walked away. As she passed the older couple, she saw them take each other's hands across the table and she smiled. That was what she wanted in life and no matter what her father said, what Liz said, what any self-help book said, it was what she deserved.

She looked at her watch as she walked out of the restaurant. Even if she had to drive all the way, she'd be in South Carolina by the time Zane got up in the morning.

Zane sat barefoot in his boxer shorts on the edge of the bed in his hotel room and stared out the window. It was still dark outside, but he could see little streaks of light just beginning to appear in the western sky. He'd been up all night, thinking. Going over and over in his mind what he had said to Ellie, what she'd said to him.

"It was her choice," he said aloud stubbornly.

The silence of the dark room was oppressive.

He missed Pops so much that it hurt. He missed Ellie even more.

"So what do you think, Pops?" he asked the empty room.

The funny thing was, suddenly he sensed he wasn't alone anymore. He smiled sadly in the darkness. He could almost feel the mattress shift as his grandfather sat down beside.

"I really screwed this one up big-time, didn't I?" He ran his hand through his bed-tousled hair. "What was wrong with me? Was I just looking for an excuse to dump her or what?"

He listened to the quiet.

"I guess I was just scared, Pops. I was upset that you were gone. That you left me. Mom left me. Dad left me. Judy left me. Maybe I thought if I sent Ellie packing, I wouldn't have to experience the pain of having her leave me, too." He gave a little laugh. "Pretty dumb, huh?"

Again, the room was quiet.

"So now what?" he said softly. "She's not going to want to talk to me. She was as afraid this wouldn't work as I was. But she's come so far in the last few months. I know you saw it, Pops."

Zane smiled at the thought of it.

"Some things were just subtle. You know, letting her hair grow out, wearing things she'd never worn before. But she was definitely learning about herself, about what she liked and didn't like. Who she really was. It took a lot of guts for her to reach out to you. To love you. It certainly took a lot of guts to stand up to Meagan."

Zane laughed and he could almost hear his grandfather chuckle.

"I guess I don't have to ask you what I should do, do I?" He turned his head and in his mind's eye, he could see Pops sitting beside him, smiling at him.

"You want to go with me?" Zane got up off the bed. "No?" He grinned. "Yeah, I made a jerk of myself in front of her, guess I have to apologize by myself, too."

He went to his suitcase and pulled out a pair of jeans and a T-shirt. "I guess Carter and Amy will understand if I miss their wedding, won't they?'' He stepped into his pants. ''Of course the whole drive back is going to be a waste of time. She's not going to want to listen to me. It's too late for apologies now. She's not going to want to marry me. Heck, I wouldn't want to marry me after the way I acted.''

Pulling his shirt over his head, he slipped into leather moccasins. ''So, I'll see you around, Pops?''

Zane felt a warmth wash over him, and he closed his eyes for a moment, lost in his grandfather's embrace.

''I'll give you a buzz, let you know if you have any great-grandchildren still in your future.''

With a smile, Zane grabbed his suitcase and walked out of his room, out of the hotel and into the early-morning light.

Elise counted the traffic lights as she drove through town. She remembered where Zane had said he'd made hotel reservations in Amy's hometown, and she'd stopped at an all night minimart to ask directions. She'd made good time driving. When Zane woke up, she planned to be camped on his doorstep. She knew he'd be angry. He might not even want to hear what she had to say, but she was going to make him listen.

Spotting the hotel sign, Elise signaled and turned her car into the parking lot. As she drove in, a car passed her.

A car that looked just like Zane's with a driver who looked remarkably like Zane....

As she passed, she turned her head to stare. It was just getting light so she couldn't see well, but she was sure it was Zane. Where was he going so early in the morning?

He turned his head at the same time and looked at her, equally surprised.

Elise pulled into the nearest parking space and cut the engine, but she held fast to the steering wheel for a minute. She was shaking all over.

Zane came around and pulled up right next to her.

She opened her car door and light flooded the pavement.

He opened the door of his rental car and she saw him, handsome good looks, tousled blond hair. He looked as if he'd just climbed out of bed...or not slept at all.

"Ellie?"

Tears filled her eyes as she walked around in front of his car in her wrinkled red suit and black designer heels that were now killing her feet. She wished she'd had the good sense to stop at a dollar store.

"What are you doing here?" Zane asked, meeting her halfway. "Didn't Lindsborg's plane make it in?"

"Zane, I'm so sorry." She reached out to him, taking both his arms, and thankfully, he didn't push her away. "You were right and I was wrong."

He rested his hands on her hips, and his touch felt so good.

"No," he said. "I was wrong. It was wrong of me to give you that kind of ultimatum. I've been in those kinds of positions before. Had I been you, I'd have done the same thing."

"You wouldn't have given up your life for the person you love just to prove a point," she whispered. "Just so you could prove yourself."

"I almost did," he answered, his blue-eyed gaze meeting hers.

"Oh, Zane," she breathed. Only she didn't try to hold back her tears. He pulled her into his arms and she hugged him tightly. "I was doing what everyone else told me to do, she said. "I was relying on them. On my father, on Liz, on Mr. Gallagher." She laughed, crying at the same time. "I even bought this stupid book telling me how to find the right husband for me. And they were wrong." She lifted her head from Zane's shoulder. "They were all wrong. I was the only one who knew who could make me happy. You made me happy."

"I should never have compared you to Judy or to my mom. I knew from the first minute I met you that you were nothing like them. Heck, Pops knew."

She laughed, sniffed and wiped her eyes.

"I'm really sorry about what I said to you about your father."

"But you were right," she murmured. "Unless I become him, just as successful, just as miserable, he's never going to accept me. But that's his problem, not mine."

Zane smiled at her and brushed her cheek with his fingertips. "You know what I figured out this morning? Well, what Pops helped me figure out?"

She shook her head, unashamed of the tears that slipped down her cheeks. "That I don't care if you're a career woman. I don't care if you want to work seven days a week, twelve hours a day. I love you, Ellie. And I'll love you any way I can get you, and if that means I have to marry the most successful real estate agent on the eastern shore, then that's just how it will have to be."

She started to laugh, then laughed harder.

He clasped her shoulders, looking down at her. "Tell me."

"Well, there may be a little problem with that." She pressed her lips together, still unable to believe she had done what she'd done. "Because I think I quit my job."

"What?"

"I realized I didn't like it," she confessed. "I don't want to work all those long hours. I don't want to miss out on all the fun in life. I don't want to miss seeing our children grow up."

"What do you want?" Zane asked, brushing her hair back with a gentle caress.

"I'm not sure yet," she said thoughtfully. "I know I want to marry you. I know I want to have your child. I think I might like to teach school, but I'd like to have some time to think about it. So how do you feel about supporting an unemployed woman?"

"I think that can be arranged." He grinned. "So Ellie Montgomery, will you marry me?"

"Only if you'll marry me, Zane Keaton."

He didn't have to answer. Instead, he took her in his arms, covered her mouth with his and kissed away any uncertainty she might have ever had that Zane was the perfect husband for her.

Epilogue

One Year Later

Elise was sitting on the porch swing snapping the last of the green beans from the garden when she saw Liz's new Mercedes convertible pull into the drive. Her friend parked under the oak tree beside Zane's pickup and followed the path up to the house, escorted by the bounding dog.

"Now don't you look a sight," Liz said. She was dressed elegantly in a pale yellow skirt and matching jacket with high heels that made those long legs of hers look like they went on forever.

Elise opened her arms to show off her rounded belly. "I'm only seven months, but I look like I'm ready to pop, don't I?"

"Oh, I don't know." Liz smiled, dropping onto the porch swing beside her. "You look pretty happy to me." She gazed down at Elise's feet, pointing. "But, *girlfriend,* that may be a little over the top."

Elise wiggled her toes and burst into laughter. "I get it—barefoot and pregnant. Well, I was the one who convinced Zane we should have a baby a year after we married—he wanted to wait. As for the shoes." She shrugged. "My feet are swollen, and it's hot in the garden."

Liz laughed and grabbed a green bean out the basket that rested between them on the swing. "I can only stay a minute because I'm showing a house down the road. I just wanted to see how you were doing."

"I'm doing great, but wish you'd come by more often," Elise said. "I miss you."

"But you don't miss work?" Liz sounded hopeful.

"Not a bit. I'm going to have the baby, hang around here for a while, and then once we're ready, I think I'd like to go to grad school."

Liz shook her head. "I still can't believe you just quit like that. Do you realize how much money you lost on the Lindsborg deal? I just bought land on the new course and contracted to have a five-bedroom, three-bath house built!"

"Lot of bathrooms to clean," Elise teased, tossing the last bean into the bowl on her lap.

Liz laughed with her as she reached to squeeze her hand. "You really are happy, aren't you?"

Elise nodded. "For me, this was the right choice for now." She rubbed her belly. "It's what I want."

Liz rose, setting the swing in motion. "Well, I have to run." She threw up her hands. "Please don't get up. You don't want to pop."

Elise laughed. "Come back soon—when you can stay."

"I will." She waved.

Just as Liz pulled out of the driveway, Zane walked up the porch steps. "Was that Liz?"

"Yeah, she was in the neighborhood, and she just stopped by to say hi." Elise stuck out her hand and Zane grasped it, helping her to her feet.

"You okay?" he asked.

She wrapped her arms around his waist. "Better than okay. I'm great."

He kissed the tip of her nose and she ran her hand over his cheek, guiding his mouth to hers. "You busy?" she murmured.

"Never too busy for you," he said huskily. "What did you have in mind?"

She lifted up on her tiptoes and whispered into his ear.

"I think I can oblige you," he teased, his voice low and sexy.

Hand in hand, Elise and Zane walked into the house, through the kitchen, down the hall past the framed *The Husband Finder* checklist and up the stairs.

One of the best things about not being a career

woman these days, Elise had learned, was that she could make love to her husband any time. She didn't know how long she would be a stay-at-home wife and mom before she joined the workforce again, but she was going to take advantage of the perks for as long as she could....

* * * * *

If you enjoyed what you just read,
then we've got an offer you can't resist!

Take 2 bestselling
love stories FREE!
Plus get a FREE surprise gift!

Clip this page and mail it to Silhouette Reader Service

IN U.S.A.	IN CANADA
3010 Walden Ave.	P.O. Box 609
P.O. Box 1867	Fort Erie, Ontario
Buffalo, N.Y. 14240-1867	L2A 5X3

YES! Please send me 2 free Silhouette Romance® novels and my free surprise gift. After receiving them, if I don't wish to receive anymore, I can return the shipping statement marked cancel. If I don't cancel, I will receive 6 brand-new novels every month, before they're available in stores! In the U.S.A., bill me at the bargain price of $21.34 per shipment plus 25¢ shipping and handling per book and applicable sales tax, if any*. In Canada, bill me at the bargain price of $24.68 plus 25¢ shipping and handling per book and applicable taxes**. That's the complete price and a savings of at least 10% off the cover prices—what a great deal! I understand that accepting the 2 free books and gift places me under no obligation ever to buy any books. I can always return a shipment and cancel at any time. Even if I never buy another book from Silhouette, the 2 free books and gift are mine to keep forever.

209 SDN DU9H
309 SDN DU9J

Name	(PLEASE PRINT)	
Address	Apt.#	
City	State/Prov.	Zip/Postal Code

* Terms and prices subject to change without notice. Sales tax applicable in N.Y.
** Canadian residents will be charged applicable provincial taxes and GST.
  All orders subject to approval. Offer limited to one per household and not valid to
  current Silhouette Romance® subscribers.
  ® are registered trademarks of Harlequin Books S.A., used under license.

SROM03   ©1998 Harlequin Enterprises Limited

SILHOUETTE *Romance*®

COMING NEXT MONTH

#1718 CATTLEMAN'S PRIDE—Diana Palmer
Long, Tall Texans
When taciturn rancher Jordan Powell made it his personal crusade to help his spirited neighbor Libby Collins hold on to her beloved homestead, everyone in Jacobsville waited with bated breath for passion to flare between these sparring partners. Could Libby accomplish what no woman had before and tame this Long, Tall Texan's restless heart?

#1719 MIDAS'S BRIDE—Myrna Mackenzie
The Brides of Red Rose
Single father Griffin O'Dell decided acquiring a palatial retreat for him and his son was much better than acquiring a wife. But the local landscaper, Abby Chesney, was not only making his home a showplace, she was making trouble! The attractive mother-to-be had already captivated Griffin's young son, and now it looked as if Griffin was next on the list!

#1720 HER MILLIONAIRE MARINE—Cathie Linz
Men of Honor
Attorney Kate Bradley had always thought Striker Kozlowski was hotter than a San Antonio summer—even after he joined the marines and his grandfather disowned him. Now the hardened soldier was back in town and temporarily running the family oil business with Kate's help. Striker didn't remember her, but she had sixty days to become someone he'd never forget....

#1721 DR. CHARMING—Judith McWilliams
Dr. Nick Balfour took one look at Gina Tesserk and realized he'd found the answer to his prayers. After all, what man wouldn't want a stunning woman tending his house? Nick hired her to work as his housekeeper until she was back on her feet. He never anticipated a few kisses with the passionate beauty would sweep him off his!

SRCNM0404